The wind died
A look of relief
thought that

"You never really get used to it," Mrs. Kinross said, indicating the destruction left by the supernatural storm. "But that one's actually happened before."

"I'm not sure it's over yet," he warned. "The temperature..."

"Yes, you're right," she said calmly. "There's probably more to come."

"Mrs. Kinross!" Wesley pointed behind her.

When she didn't move, he tackled her, waist high, driving her to the kitchen floor. She screamed.

But the meat cleaver that he had seen levitating from her wooden knife block sailed harmlessly over them and slammed into the wall instead of into her skull, which is where it had been headed.

Of course, now the other knives were on the move....

Angel™

City Of
Not Forgotten
Redemption
Close to the Ground
Shakedown
Hollywood Noir
Avatar
Soul Trade
Bruja
The Summoned
Haunted
Image
Stranger to the Sun
Vengeance
Endangered Species
The Longest Night, Vol. 1
Impressions
Sanctuary
Fearless
Solitary Man

Angel: The Casefiles, Vol. 1—The Official Companion
The Essential Angel Posterbook

Available from Pocket Books

ANGEL™

solitary man

Jeff Mariotte

**An original novel based on the television series
created by Joss Whedon & David Greenwalt**

POCKET BOOKS

New York　London　Toronto　Sydney　Singapore

Historian's note: This story takes place during the first half of the fourth season of *Angel*.

This book is a work of fiction. Any references to historical events, real people, or real locales are used fictitiously. Other names, characters, places, and incidents are the product of the author's imagination, and any resemblance to actual events or locales or persons, living or dead, is entirely coincidental.

First POCKET BOOKS edition December 2003

Copyright © 2003 by Twentieth Century Fox, Inc.
All Rights Reserved

POCKET BOOKS
An imprint of Simon & Schuster
Africa House
64–78 Kingsway
London WC2B 6AH

www.simonsays.co.uk

All rights reserved, including the right of
reproduction in whole or in part in any form.

The text of this book was set in New Caledonia.
Printed and Bound in Great Britain by Cox & Wyman Ltd
10 9 8 7 6 5 4 3 2 1

A CIP catalogue record for this book is available from
the British Library
ISBN 0-7434-7796-0

There is an enormous contingent of *Angel* fans out there, online and otherwise. Additionally, there are mystery fans, horror fans, and people who consider themselves fans of virtually every type of entertainment. You guys give us the energy to keep going. This one's for all of you.

Writing a book can be a solitary experience, so it's nice to be able to reach out to friends and family, including Maryelizabeth, Holly, Dave, and Tara. Thanks as always to Lisa Clancy and Lisa Gribbin of Simon & Schuster, Debbie Olshan at Fox, everyone at Mutant Enemy, and the cast of *Angel*.

CHAPTER ONE

Mildred Finster closed the book and held it in her small hands for a moment before setting it down gently on the side table, next to a cooling cup of tea and a porcelain angel strumming a golden harp. She let out a soft sigh as she did so, and Pookie—a sleek Persian the color of wood smoke, with pale golden eyes—regarded her with an inquisitive gaze. "That's the last Agatha Christie novel," Mildred explained to the cat. "Seventy-nine books, and I've now read them all."

Pookie expressed his commiseration with a quiet "mrrawrr," twitched his tail once, and curled up on the carpet near Mildred's slippered feet. Mildred knew her situation wasn't as dire as she made it sound. Agatha Christie had always been her favorite, but there were plenty of other writers whose work she admired. Dorothy L. Sayers, of course, and Margery Allingham and Ngaio Marsh, and of more recent vintage Donna Andrews and Carolyn Hart, were all favorites. And once in a while, as a special challenge, she picked up a John Dickson Carr. She loved books in which the puzzle tested even her abilities to the utmost, and there were a number of writers she'd given up on simply because they'd lost the ability to fool her. But there was a good mystery bookstore not far from her Pasadena home, and they kept her well supplied.

Still, she thought, *the last Christie. That has special significance.* And she had saved *Curtain* till the end because it was the last novel Christie wrote, and she knew that in it Christie had killed off her Belgian sleuth, Hercule Poirot, who was Mildred's favorite detective. She sighed again, causing Pookie to twitch his back the way cats did. She had known this day would come eventually—if one lived long enough, she had learned, all the sad ones did, as well as a reasonable number of the other kind—but now that it was here it was even worse than she had anticipated.

After sitting for a few moments in the sorrowful afterglow of Poirot's final curtain, she put her hands on the armrests of her chair and pushed herself to her feet, careful not to step on Pookie as she did so. In seventy-one years, life had taught her many lessons, some of them difficult ones indeed, and one of them was that, no matter what, life went on. Dealing with it, going about one's business, getting on with things—these had a tendency to dissipate the sadness even of the worst events, like the death of her husband, Philip, eight years before. Certainly a little activity would push aside the fragile web of gloom that enveloped her after finishing the book.

And she knew just what she meant to do. There was a business card in her kitchen somewhere—that was where she kept all her important paperwork—and she just had to find it. She clicked off her reading lamp, and leaving Pookie on the carpet in front of her reading chair, carried her teacup into the kitchen, rinsed it in the sink, set it on the yellow tiled countertop, and began the search.

The first place she looked was on the corkboard she kept on the wall by the telephone. She found emergency phone numbers; cards for a plumber, an electrician, and Pookie's vet; a list of local library branches and their hours of operation; but the card she was looking for wasn't there. There was, however, a receipt for work that had been done on her Dodge, and she couldn't imagine why that was still up there, since it had been a couple of months and the car was running fine now, so she pulled it off the board and put it in the deep drawer where she filed such things. Then she searched inside the drawer, in which she kept careful records of household expenses, files of grocery coupons, bills waiting to be paid, and other necessary paperwork.

ANGEL

These papers were rigidly organized, and the card she sought was not among them.

The two likeliest spots ruled out, Mildred Finster felt her mood already lifting. This was turning into a puzzle, and if there was one thing she loved, it was a puzzle. *Where would I,* she wondered, *have put that card?* Someplace secure, someplace where it wouldn't accidentally be thrown away or turned over and used as scratch paper. She checked her wallet, and she checked the refrigerator, where magnets held recipes and drawings by her nephew Hank's young children. Finally a flash of inspiration struck her and she went back through her parlor and down the hall to her bedroom, where open curtains allowed the late afternoon sunshine to illuminate the collection of porcelain angels that guarded the top of her dresser. On the nightstand next to her bed were a couple of books. Both were short story collections, because before going to sleep she liked to read a single story from start to finish, and while one of them had a real bookmark holding her place, the other had a smudged, dog-eared rectangle of heavy paper. It was the business card, which she had found stuck at the corner of a shop window as if it had been blown there by a stray breeze. She had kept it because she liked angels and she liked mystery stories, and this single piece of paper seemed to combine her two interests.

She found an unused bookmark in the nightstand's drawer, the kind with a ribbon and a little angel dangling at the end, and put it in the book in place of the card. Then she turned the card around and read its face, even though she had done so dozens of times already. There was an odd drawing on it that she had at first thought showed a man's bowtie under a collar button, but that the business name on the card had clarified for her. "Angel Investigations," it said, and there was a Hollywood phone number underneath that. Curious, she had called the number when she'd first found the card and, after pretending that she had need of a private detective, had been given an address. She had written the address down on the face of the card, but had never followed up in any other way because she did not, in fact, need a detective.

What she needed was to become one.

She had Pookie and her books and a few remaining friends to fill her days. She and Philip had both worked for years, and between both pensions and insurance—Philip had been a thirty-year man with the good hands people and had always carried plenty of coverage—money wasn't a problem for her. Physically she was in good shape—okay, not as good as she had been in days gone by, but who was, at seventy-one? Still, she could get around without a cane, she could drive, and with her glasses on her eyesight was fine. She was sharp and observant and well educated, and she had a knack, proven dozens of times over, for solving mysteries. How different could the real-life ones be?

Actually, she suspected, they were *very* different. Which was why she couldn't just get a license and call herself a detective. She had done some research and learned that she needed to apprentice with an existing firm, put in a set number of hours required by California's licensing law, and get some real investigative experience under her belt. Then she could hang her shingle and spend her golden years helping those in need and putting her puzzle-solving skills to good use.

She'd read the Mrs. Pollifax mysteries, of course, but they were just stories. The CIA wouldn't hire a woman in her seventies to help them on cases. That's why she needed her own agency—after the legally required apprenticeship, of course, since she had always been a law-abiding woman—so she could set her own rules.

Mildred sat down on her bed and tugged off her slippers. *There's no time like the present,* she thought. She didn't care for night driving, but there were still a couple hours of sunlight left, and no particular obligations weighed on her. Twenty minutes later, dressed in a neat pantsuit, her white clutch purse in her hand, she bade good-bye to Pookie and headed for her car, and Hollywood.

• • •

Charles Gunn thought that if he lived to be a hundred—hell, if he lived to be as old as Angel—he would still never fully understand the mind and heart of Winifred Burkle. He'd thought they were close, that he was getting to know her as well as he had ever known anyone. But that had all changed in one horrible instant. The worst part was, he had done Fred an enormous favor, or at least that was the way he saw it. He had allowed her the peace of knowing that the weasel who had been responsible for her five years of torment in Pylea could never hurt her, or anyone else on Earth, again. He had spared her from the cost—which he knew, from hard experience, was almost too high to bear—of taking her own revenge. He had added one more life to his own pile of burdens in order to keep her from having to carry it.

He hadn't really expected her to be grateful—that just wasn't Fred. But her reaction had been even more severe than he could have guessed. She had turned Arctic, as if he had betrayed her in some awful way. If he *had* betrayed her, at least he would understand her reaction. And because honor was important to him, he would agree that he deserved the punishment. He hadn't betrayed her, though. He had done her a solid, and her punishment was way out of proportion to the crime.

They moved around each other in the Hyperion

ANGEL

Hotel like eggshell-walkers, Gunn especially cautious because the slightest wrong word or phrasing could earn him a cutting glare or a frown guaranteed to spoil his day. They had hardly touched since the incident; although they still slept in the same bed, Fred pulled herself into a tight ball and gave off porcupine vibes that kept him at bay. He felt an overwhelming urge to hit something, to batter some demon or vamp until his knuckles were raw and bloody. But for the past several days the supernatural world had been quiet. Too quiet, Lorne had opined, dusting off the old cliché about the calm before the storm. So Gunn stayed close to the hotel, and therefore to Fred, and stewed, and the anxiety within him stayed there with no outlet.

That was why, when the front door scraped open and a little old lady who could only be a potential client walked in, blinking uncertainly at the big lobby, he practically jumped from his chair. She was a tiny white woman, probably little more than five feet tall and a hundred pounds, dressed in a purple jacket and pants with a neat white blouse. A small round locket hung around her neck on a fine gold chain, and she gripped a little white leather purse. If it hadn't been for the purple she'd have looked like a snow-woman.

"Something I can help you with, ma'am?" he asked.

She hesitated a moment before she answered, and he worried that she actually was looking for a hotel room instead of an investigative agency. That, he couldn't help her with. But she glanced down at a card in her free hand and said, "Is this . . . is this Angel Investigations?"

He allowed himself a smile. *At last, something to do.* He guessed the card in her hand was one of the second generation of their business cards—the first version had only contained Cordy's angel drawing and a phone number, but when they had moved to the hotel they'd added the name because too many people misinterpreted the sketch. "You bet," he told her. "What's your problem? Ghouls? Hellbeasts?"

Before the woman could answer, he felt Fred coming up behind him: her movement stirring the air ever so slightly, her footfall soft as the beat of a butterfly's wing, her scent rising around him like fog. "He's always joking around like that," Fred said, her faint Texas accent almost imperceptibly drawing out her words. "How can we help you, ma'am?"

"This *is* a detective agency?" the woman asked, still sounding uncertain and maybe a little nervous now.

"That it is," Gunn assured her. "Detecting is what we do. We can detect like crazy. Just turn us loose and watch us detect."

The old woman returned his smile now. Or maybe it was Fred's smile she was returning. Part of him wanted to check and see if Fred was, in fact, smiling, but the other part of him knew that her smile, right now, had the power to break his heart all over again. So he didn't look at her, but kept his eyes instead focused on the woman. "I don't really need any detecting done, thank you," she told them. "My name is Mildred Finster. I would like to work here."

"Work?" Gunn echoed, not quite sure he'd actually heard her correctly. "What . . . kind of work, exactly?"

"I want to be an apprentice detective," she explained. "I want to work for an agency until I have enough hours to get licensed as a private investigator."

Licensed? Gunn thought. *Is this some kind of trap?* He was pretty sure that Angel Investigations wasn't licensed by anyone. California required licenses to drive, to carry concealed weapons, and to hunt or fish, but he wasn't sure they had a demon-whomping licensing department.

"I don't think we're exactly hiring right now," he told her, sorry that he'd jumped up to greet her in the first place. Fred was better with loonies than he was. She'd been half loony herself when they'd met her in Pylea, so she had that natural sympathy for them.

"No, we're not," Fred interjected. "And our

cases aren't very typical, either. I'm sure there are lots of other agencies that would be better suited to your requirements."

Mildred Finster looked crestfallen. "But this one is so convenient to home," she insisted. "I'm just a couple of blocks from the 110, and then it's an easy transition onto the 101 and right into Hollywood. And I love angels—you'd be surprised if you saw my house; I have at least a hundred of the little china ones, you know, with the rosy cheeks. I looked in the phone book but the other ones all have such grim-sounding names. California Investigative Services; Moore and Fitch, Investigators; Affiliated Security Systems, Inc. I'd be bored to tears just answering the phone. Angel Investigations sounds so welcoming, so pleasant and cheerful, like you really are peoples' guardian angels, watching over them and helping with their problems. And you're both such nice young people. I promise I wouldn't be a bother, and I'm really very good at solving puzzles. Go ahead, try me."

"Try you?"

"Give me a puzzle to solve. One of your cases, anything."

"We don't really work that way, ma'am," Fred told her. Gunn figured Fred had a handle on the situation and he moved back, letting her take care of things. If she needed him he'd be within earshot.

"But you do solve cases, right? Mysteries?"

"Well, yes, but—," Fred began.

The older woman cut her off. "Well, then, that's what I'm looking for. Someplace where I can put my skills to use helping people."

How are your staking skills? Gunn wondered. *Dusted any bloodsuckers lately? Decapitated any slime demons?* He was sure that Mildred Finster meant well, but equally certain that she had no idea what kind of investigations they actually did here.

As if to put her to the ultimate test, Gunn heard a booming voice coming from one of the back offices, and getting closer. "Oh, Fred," Lorne's singsong tones called. "Have you been using the Ankhnaten Grimoire, peanut, because I need to look—"

Gunn moved quickly to intercept Lorne at the doorway before he stepped out and revealed himself to Mildred Finster in all his green-skinned, red-eyed, Italian-silk-suited glory. He put a hand out and pressed it against Lorne's chest, driving him back into the office he was coming out of.

"It's in here," he said. "I'm sure I saw it."

"No, darlin', I've looked," Lorne argued. "It's not—"

Gunn jerked his head toward the lobby. "Civilian," he hissed. "Of the way elderly persuasion. You might give her a heart attack or somethin'."

Lorne's eyes lit up as he got the message. "Got

it, Mr. Clean," he said, making his daily reference to Gunn's smooth pate. "What's the case? Demonic possession? Blood running from the faucets? I love that one."

"No case," Gunn told him. "One of the Golden Girls wants a job here."

"Is it Bea Arthur?" Lorne asked, sounding hopeful. "Because I've always admired her work so much." He chuckled softly. "That Maude . . ."

"Look, just stay in here till she leaves," Gunn suggested. "Fred's tryin' to get rid of her, and then she won't run away all freaked out because she saw the jolly green giant in here. I want to stay close in case she turns out to be a shapeshifter in disguise or something, but I'm thinkin' that's not likely. Looks like the genuine article to me."

Lorne looked despondent, although Gunn suspected he was faking it. "Sure, lock me away like the insane aunt in the attic," he said. "I'll be okay in here. I'm sure there are vermin to eat."

Gunn chuckled. "It's only for a minute, dog. Just hang tight."

"Hanging," Lorne assured him. Gunn went back into the lobby just in time to hear Fred dismissing the woman once and for all.

"I'm sorry we couldn't be more helpful to you, ma'am. Good luck finding a position somewhere else."

"Well, thank you for your time, young lady,"

Mildred Finster replied. "You're just as sweet and cute as a gumdrop."

"Or one of those plastic bears with the honey inside," Gunn offered. "That's what I always tell her."

Mildred laughed, and he noticed that the lines on her face seemed to melt away when she did so. *That was one fine-looking woman in her time,* he thought. *Fred will look that good when she's that age. Or better.*

But when he turned to catch Fred's eye, he realized that he might not be part of her life by then. The honey bear comment, instead of endearing him to her, had been taken in entirely the wrong way and she was staring daggers at him. Without saying a word, Fred turned away from him and went back to whatever she had been doing before. Mildred Finster left the hotel, and Gunn felt like he was alone on a glacier.

That could have gone better, Mildred thought. Those young people had been just as nice as could be, if a little strange. And she wished she'd been able to meet the man with the wonderfully musical voice she'd heard in the other room. She understood that it was a lot to expect, that the first place she tried—and with such a perfect name—would have an apprenticeship slot available exactly when she was looking. And she knew, too, that most agencies that might be willing to take on an apprentice would be looking for someone a few years younger. But the fact remained, she was as well suited to detective work as anyone, regardless of age. Maybe better than some. Detectives, she figured, had to blend in to various situations without being noticed, or suspected. Anyone would notice those two young people, both so bright and attractive. But who would suspect Mildred Finster of anything? She could stake out anyplace without arousing undue attention.

She couldn't blame them, though. They didn't know that. As far as they were concerned, she was probably just a slightly dotty old woman with a crazy idea in her head.

There had to be a way to disabuse them of that notion.

CHAPTER TWO

Hair still wet from his shower, Angel headed for the staircase that led down to the hotel's lobby. There were aspects of being a vampire that he was fine with—he'd long ago gotten past any queasiness about surviving on blood, though these days he got his from friendly butchers instead of unwilling victims. He actually liked the increased strength and stamina and the heightened senses—he couldn't have done the things he did without them, in fact. The part about not being out in sunlight was kind of a pain, but growing up in Ireland, tanning had never really been a priority, and even though he'd been in California these last few decades, he knew that people with dark tans were risking skin cancer anyway—not as immediate a dilemma as bursting into flames, but still something one had to keep in mind.

But not having a reflection—that was an ongoing

problem. He tried to keep his hair mostly low-maintenance. But partially because of the sunlight thing, he spent a lot of time traveling through sewers. And the kinds of places supernatural baddies hung out tended not to be the most sterile locations either. Angel tried to stay clean, showered regularly, but if he picked up an oil stain on his cheek or a smudge on his nose—or even, as had happened a couple of days ago when he was making some notes, a Sharpie streak across his chin—unless someone told him about it he was completely unaware.

And they didn't call Sharpies "permanent" markers for nothing, as it turned out. That had taken scrubbing after scrubbing, each time going to Lorne to find out if he had washed it all away.

He felt clean now, but as he came downstairs into a room where the tension was almost palpable, he thought that maybe another shower—one that would last until his teammates all solved for themselves whatever personal issues they had going on—would be a good idea. Something had happened between Gunn and Fred, throwing a giant-size monkey wrench into their budding romance. They sat at separate desks, backs to each other, not speaking. Before whatever happened had happened, they would have been sitting together; even if involved in different tasks, their knees would have been touching, or their shoulders, and there would have been frequent pauses to discuss their progress. They would, at the least, have stolen glances and the occasional kiss.

Gunn noticed him first. "Hey, Angel," he said.

Then Fred looked up. "You missed a visitor," she reported cheerfully. "She wanted to be your apprentice."

"An apprentice vampire?"

"No, silly, an apprentice detective. She must have been at least seventy years old."

Angel smiled. "Did she have her own magnifying glass and trench coat? Because if she does I might be able to use her."

"I think all she had was ambition," Fred replied.

"And the investigative chops to find us," Gunn added. "Since we ain't exactly big on advertising, that's something, right?"

Lorne came out of an inner office then, an exaggerated frown on his face. "Gunn wouldn't even let me meet her," the Pylean demon said. "As if my appearance would be scarier to the little old lady from Pasadena than his own tough-guy urban street demeanor."

"How did you know she was from Pasadena?" Fred asked, surprised.

"I didn't, nugget," he answered. "It's just a song. Before your time."

She'd lived on Earth a lot longer than Lorne had, Angel knew. But when it came to music—which wasn't allowed back in Lorne's home dimension—he had proven to be a fast learner. He knew more about music than any ten humans Angel had ever met, and he retained it all.

Lorne's good humor was infectious, and his entry into the lobby had helped to defray the tension there. Fred and Gunn, Angel noted, were participating in the same conversation without speaking directly to each other, which was strange. But at least they were all talking, and the room wasn't as grave-silent as it had been. He liked it when the big lobby was filled with the sounds of voices. Happy voices, preferably.

And then, Angel thought as the hotel's front door opened and she swept in, *there's Cordelia.*

"Hi, guys," she said. She seemed upbeat enough, but it was hard to tell with her these days. She had been through experiences she couldn't even fully describe to Angel—elevated to more-or-less godhood, then returned to Earth but with no memory. Angel had come to the conclusion, just before her disappearance—and his own involuntary incarceration in a tiny cage at the bottom of the ocean—that he loved Cordelia Chase. He was pretty sure she felt the same way.

But without her memory she hadn't even known for sure if he was a friend, much less a lover. He knew that, until she had rediscovered her own feelings, he couldn't force anything on her, couldn't expect her to declare a love that he suspected was there but of which he had no definitive proof. And once her memory had finally been returned to her, she'd been confused, in a vulnerable emotional state. Instead of staying at the hotel, where Angel might have been able to press his case, to influence her, she had chosen to stay with his son, Connor. *My estranged son, Connor,* he thought. Or *should that just be "strange" son?* He shook his head. The whole situation was just too complicated to think about, especially with Cordy walking toward him across the lobby floor, a hesitant smile on her beautiful face. All he wanted to do was rush to her with his arms open and envelop her, never let her go.

"Is this a bad time?" Cordy asked. Angel figured that whatever expression had been on his face, it hadn't been the right one, hadn't been welcoming, or loving, or something.

"No, it's fine, it's good," Angel said quickly. "How are you?"

She came closer but stopped out of arm's reach. Her eyes met his only briefly and then she flashed a bright smile at everyone else. But when she spoke, she looked toward the floor. "I'm sorry to come in like this when there's a problem," she began.

"What problem?" Angel countered anxiously. "There's no problem."

"Yes, there is," Cordy said. "I've had a vision."

"Are you okay?" he asked. There had been a time when the visions were physically devastating to her. Lately they had seemed few and far between, which he took to be another sign of her change from merely human to something else altogether.

"Yeah," she replied. "I'm fine, nothing to it. But, you know, vision, someone in nasty ooky trouble. They kind of go together."

"What's the haps, honeybunch?" Lorne asked her. He did go to her, gave a hug, and got one in return. Angel wished he could do the same, without it being all complicated. "Don't keep the bad news all to yourself."

"It was a strange one," she said with a half-smile. "Not that they're not usually pretty strange. But even by usual standards, this one . . . well, I saw this truck driver. A big, burly guy, you know, the kind who has muscles on his muscles. And he was being threatened, in my vision, by . . . well, by what looked like a perfectly nice little old man."

"What is it, geriatric week around here?" Gunn asked. "I'm startin' to hear Lawrence Welk music in my head. And I don't even know any Lawrence Welk music."

"Geriatrics? Did I miss something?" Cordelia said. Then a bit of her old mischievousness returned to light up her eyes and she added, "Or are we just talking about Angel?"

"Never mind," Angel prompted. "What about

this old man? What is he, some kind of demon? Or a vampire?"

"I couldn't really tell," Cordelia replied. "Just that he was some kind of danger to the truck driver, unlikely as that sounds. I would have called, but, you know, Connor's place doesn't exactly have phone service, and I was headed this way anyhow."

Angel chose to take that as a good sign—that she came to the hotel because she wanted to be with him, or at least with them, the only real family she had any more. And she'd left Connor behind at his place. Angel truly loved his son, but the boy was a loose cannon—powerful and unpredictable, with loyalties that wavered like a politician's principles the week before election day.

"Do you know where this attack is going to take place?" Fred asked Cordy.

"Yes, I was able to pinpoint a location from a sign I saw. It's a truck stop. Kind of out in the boonies, though. Way out, actually."

"Then we'd better get going," Angel said. "Let's move."

Mildred Finster keyed the engine of her Dodge Dart to life when she saw the long black car emerge from the hotel's parking area. The car—a convertible, she noted, though the roof was up—was even older than her own. A man she hadn't seen before was at the wheel. The nice young black man and the girl with the long dark hair were in the backseat, and sitting next to the driver was the lovely young lady who had entered through the front door just a few moments before.

She gave the black car time to get down the block, then turned on her headlights, switched on her blinker, and pulled out into the lane. She followed at a distance of several car lengths. If they were worried about being followed, they might be able to spot her, but she thought she could stay back far enough to keep them in sight without making herself too obvious. She had filled her gas tank before heading into Hollywood, so if they didn't go too far she should be able to keep up.

A little thrill tickled through her at the realization that she was actually following another car. She had no idea where they were going—maybe on a case, maybe just out to supper—but when she proved to them that she could surreptitiously keep tabs on them, they'd have to recognize her potential value to their agency. As the black car charged up a freeway on-ramp, Mildred pressed down on her own gas pedal and felt the Dodge respond accordingly.

She had just gotten started, but already this detective business was a kick!

The truck stop Cordelia's vision led them to was almost an hour away, in El Monte. It consisted of a coffee shop, a gift and supply store, showers, and a truck wash, surrounded by a vast tarmac on which were parked dozens of big rigs, travel trailers, and private autos.

And in one section near the edge of the tarmac, where it bordered what looked like miles of ungroomed scrub, several police cars and an ambulance were parked. This area was sealed off by yellow crime scene tape, and cops wandered here and there or stood in small groups, talking in quiet tones. Crime scene investigators paced off the area, took photographs, and stood small yellow A-frame cards with numbers on them beside bits of evidence that Angel couldn't see from where he had stopped his car. Even with the windows rolled up he could hear the rumble of the generators powering the arc lights that washed the crime scene with brilliant illumination.

"Looks like we're too late," Angel said, glancing at Cordy. "You're sure this is the right place?"

"It's the right truck stop," Cordelia replied with certainty. "I don't know for sure if those police officers are looking at the body of the trucker I saw—I'd have to get in there and see him to be sure—but I have a bad feeling that they might be."

Angel shared that bad feeling. "Why don't you and I get closer?" he suggested. "You guys stay here by the car." Gunn and Fred had been virtually silent all the way out, each hugging his or her respective door and letting a wall of tension sit between them. Angel had left Lorne back at the hotel, just because even at a California truck stop, the sight of a tall horned demon with green skin might attract unwanted notice.

"We can try to," Cordy agreed. She opened her door and got out. Angel did the same. Gunn grunted his assent and left the car only to lean against it, arms crossed, face clouded.

"Maybe they'll work out their problems while they're here," Angel whispered to Cordy as they crossed the tarmac. Despite the cool evening, the air was thick with the stink of diesel fumes.

"And maybe we'll come back to find only one of them standing," Cordy countered. "My money's on Fred. Gunn's got the strength but I bet she fights dirty when the chips are down."

She sounded like the old Cordy when she said that, and Angel tossed her a grin. In another few moments they were at the area demarcated by the yellow tape. One of the cops shot them a questioning look.

"Hey, what's going on?" Angel asked, trying to sound friendly and curious.

"Police business," the cop replied flatly. "Nothing to see here."

"There's gotta be something, right?" Angel insisted. "Somebody get hurt? If there's a problem, we got a right to know. I don't want my wife"—he ticked his eyes toward Cordelia, but saw no reaction on her face—"to be in any danger around here."

"No danger," the cop said reluctantly. "There's been a truck stolen. Guy who did it is miles away. But trucks have GPS, clear markings—we'll find it in no time. Nothing to worry about."

"Anybody hurt?" Angel asked again. "When the truck was stolen?"

"What are you, Geraldo Rivera?" the cop shot back, angry now at Angel's insistent questioning. "I told you all I'm going to."

Cordelia elbowed her way past Angel. "You'll have to excuse him," she said. "He doesn't really play well with others. It's been a problem since kindergarten. What he means is, we're concerned about the driver because . . . well, you know, man's inhumanity to man is so out of control these days, and—"

"Look, lady," the cop said with finality, "I'm not telling you anything I didn't tell your husband. Why don't you both just get back in your car and move on down the road?"

They were, Angel knew, at an impasse. There were ways to find out more, but they wouldn't make any progress right now, not with all these cops around. He shrugged and tossed a fake smile at the cop. "Thanks for your help," he said, and turned on his heel, tugging Cordy away with him.

They had only taken a few steps away from the scene when they saw an elderly woman tottering toward the tape, her face a mask of fear. "It's Jack, isn't it?" Angel heard her cry. "It's my baby!"

Oh, no, he thought. *Telling the next of kin must be the worst part of the job, but having a grieving mother show up at the scene would have to be even harder.* He felt terrible for the woman, and for the cops who would have to deal with her.

But when they got back to the GTX Gunn and Fred were both laughing hysterically. "What's the joke?" he wondered.

"That lady," Gunn managed, but then he was gripped by a paroxysm of laughter and couldn't finish.

"That's her," Fred said through her own tears of laughter. "Your would-be apprentice."

"She's the driver's mother," Angel said, confused.

"No, she's not," Gunn argued. "She's gotta be faking it. That's the woman that came to the hotel today lookin' for a job."

"You're kidding," Cordelia said. "That's why you made the geriatric crack? She wanted to work for Angel Investigations?"

"She wants to be an *apprentice* detective," Fred explained. "Until she can open her own agency."

Now Cordelia started to laugh too, looking back toward the crime scene. There were several officers gathered around the woman, and it looked like they were all talking at once. "She's probably getting more information than we did, Angel," she said. "Maybe you should hire her after all."

Angel had a hard time seeing the humor in the situation. "She can have my job," he said grumpily.

They waited there, by the car, and after a few minutes of talking to the police—Angel noted that they even let her under the yellow tape and escorted her to the edge of the tarmac, where presumably she could see whatever the cops were keeping from public view, at the fringes of the scrubland—the old woman came back toward them. Now there was a sly smile on her face instead of the near-panic Angel had seen there before.

When she reached them she approached Gunn and Fred and launched into a recitation. Angel caught a whiff of some floral scent from her—a dry perfume or eau de toilette that had been applied maybe a tad too generously. "I told them I thought my son Jack had been hurt," she explained. "Of course, Philip and I were never blessed with children, but they don't know that, do they? So they had to convince me that it wasn't Jack, which they did by showing me the body and telling me his name. Apparently he still had his billfold on him, with identification. His name is Cal Barnett. He's from Sacramento, and he drives for the Crossways Freight company, and—"

"Was there a description of the suspect?" Angel interrupted, still trying to make sure that this murder was the friendly-old-man attack that Cordy had seen in her vision.

"Excuse me, young man," the woman said tartly. "I'm talking to your employers."

"My . . . ," Angel began.

Gunn laughed. "No, ma'am. That's Angel. *The* Angel, of Angel Investigations."

The woman's cheeks crimsoned. "Oh, I'm so sorry. I thought the name was just metaphorical; I didn't realize there was an actual person named Angel."

"More or less," Fred put in.

"That's all right," Angel assured her. "Not a problem."

"Well, then, I suppose I should answer your question, after all, Mr. Angel. I apologize for my rudeness. My name is Mildred Finster, and I met these two earlier today," the woman said. "And the answer is, no, nobody saw the attack. But the aftermath is horrible. There's so much blood. . . . Is this a regular thing, for you? Seeing these kinds of horrors?"

"You'd be surprised at the stuff we see," Gunn told her.

"That's really all I was able to find out, I'm afraid," she went on. "His name, the company he works for—the truck is missing, stolen, they said, and I don't know what the cargo is. Well, that and the fact that he's from Sacramento and not my 'Jack' at all."

"Still better than we did," Cordelia admitted.

Fred, suddenly serious, stepped forward and took Mildred's hands in her own. "Ms. Finster, you've been a big help and we really appreciate it," she said thoughtfully. "But now that you've seen the victim, I hope you realize how dangerous this business can be. We're trained professionals, and sometimes it's still hard for us. It really isn't a business that amateurs can afford to get mixed up in, okay?"

"I appreciate your concern, dear," Mildred Finster responded. "I have to admit, it was a bit of a fright, seeing the poor man like that. A mystery has to have a body, I suppose, but in the books they usually seem quite a bit tidier." She brightened up a little and shared a smile. "But it certainly has been exciting. It's a pleasure to meet all of you, truly it is. I'll get out of your way now and let you professionals carry on. Toodle-oo."

As he watched her walk toward her own car, Angel didn't know quite what to think of Mildred Finster. But whoever she was, whatever she was about, she'd been more effective here than he had.

That fact, he realized, kind of worried him.

CHAPTER THREE

Crossways Freight's Los Angeles headquarters was in an industrial neighborhood called City of Commerce. That name, and the nearby City of Industry, had always struck Angel as perversely humorous—what American city didn't include industry and commerce? Most of them at least made an attempt to appeal to humans, too, but those two towns seemed to have given up on the human element altogether. He couldn't imagine intentionally living in such a place.

The Crossways building filled its own block, mostly with a big yard for trucks, loading docks, and warehouse facilities. Angel sat on the roof of a building across the street and watched it for a while. It seemed never to close, with trucks rumbling in and out even in the darkness. But the front of the building, where he suspected its offices were probably located, was quiet and unlit at this time of night.

ANGEL

That's good enough for me, he thought after twenty minutes of surveillance. He leaped down from his perch, landed on the street three stories below, took a few running steps, and jumped up again. His powerful legs propelled him high into the air, and he touched down lightly on the flat roof of the Crossways offices. This single-story front section of the building jutted out from the larger and taller warehouse section, which had a corrugated steel roof. Landing on that would have made a thunderous racket, but in front the roof was pebbled and studded with air conditioning and ventilation units, and landing quietly was no big trick.

Angel made a quick survey of the possible ways inside from there. Going through the ducts was one option, though he preferred to keep that as a last resort. A better answer presented itself momentarily, though—a ventilation grate that passed into the warehouse, built into the wall that rose up from this roof to the warehouse's higher one. Angel pried two of the slats apart and looked inside. There was activity back at the loading docks, but he couldn't see any on this end of the cavernous space. With his fingers he yanked out the bolts holding the grate in place, freed it from the wall, and set it down gingerly on the roof. Slipping through it, he grabbed some electrical conduits on the other side and lowered himself down. When he was just a dozen feet from the floor he stopped and waited, checking again to make sure the area was still clear. Seeing that it was, he dropped the rest of the way, landing lightly on the balls of his feet.

A simple wooden door was all that stood between him and the offices now. The knob was locked but Angel snapped the lock with one twist of his wrist and passed inside.

Moonlight streamed in through windows, and a couple of hall lights had been left on, but otherwise this side of the building was as dark and empty as Angel had anticipated. He felt a little bad about breaking in—he doubted very much that the trucking company had done anything wrong; they had been victimized, here, by the assault on their driver and the theft of their truck and cargo. But he also knew that they would never cooperate with his search, particularly since a crime had been committed. If he was going to help he needed to know as much as he could, and simply asking questions wasn't going to get him anywhere. So he broke in. Now he just needed to help himself to the information.

The only problem was, he didn't quite know where to start.

He wandered around the maze of offices until he found a dispatcher's, with huge, minutely detailed maps of California and other western states on the walls, flanked by a monolithic bank of filing cabinets. He checked under "B" for Barnett, the truck driver's name, but quickly found that the files weren't arranged that way. They did contain bills of lading, but they were organized numerically. Angel looked around for some way to determine the ID numbers on Barnett's truck, but the only possibility that presented itself was the computer on the dispatcher's desk.

Angel had never particularly liked computers. He was more comfortable with them than he had once been, but he still wasn't exactly a fan. He wished for a moment that he had Cordy here to help. Then he wished he just had Cordy here, in this dark, quiet place, so they could . . . He pushed that thought out of his head before it distracted him any more, and booted up the computer. When it came on, he sat down at the desk and started poking through its hard drive, searching for Cal Barnett's name.

Finally he found it, and with it a schedule. Barnett tended to make trips up and down the coast, not leaving the state, and usually wasn't away from home for more than a few nights. On this trip he'd been coming from a State Parks Department storehouse in Red Bluff, at the northern end of the state. The driver had been very near his final destination, in Chino. He must have stopped for gas, or a cup of coffee, before going those last few miles.

Maybe he had been too sleepy to continue, or maybe he'd just needed a pit stop. But the decision had cost him his life. Angel copied down the address on a piece of scratch paper and tucked it in his pocket.

With the schedule came the truck's identification numbers, so he was able to go back to the filing cabinet and pull the bill of lading. Angel scanned the list of items the truck was carrying. It was an odd combination of things—benches, altars, crucifixes, a pulpit, candelabras, bells, various statuary, several baptismal fonts, a few large kettles, and more traditional furniture of various descriptions, including desks and beds. The list was a long one, but Angel didn't see anything on it worth killing for.

"But somebody *is* dead," Cordelia complained. "That truck driver I saw, Cal Barnett. So *someone* thinks the truck is worth killing for."

Angel had returned to the hotel and met up with the rest of the team there, reporting what he'd found in the Crossways Freight office. He had already come to the same conclusion Cordelia had, but still didn't have any answers beyond that.

"What I don't understand," Fred brought up, "and maybe it's just because I don't always follow all The Powers That Be stuff, but why would you have had a vision, Cordelia, if it was too late to do anything about it? I mean, by the time we got there the poor guy was already dead. We couldn't have made it any faster unless we'd had superpowers, or an Angel-copter or something."

"I'm not sure about that either," Cordy admitted. "Usually the whole point of the visions is to be able to save whoever is in trouble. And like I said, the whole vision thing is almost ancient history at this point, so I don't know why this one was important enough to send me."

"I've been practically pulling my horns out over that one, kiddies," Lorne said. "And I've only been able to come up with one plausible explanation. One that, I'm not afraid to say, I don't like even one little bit."

Fred turned to him with a quizzical look. "What is it, Lorne?"

"It's always bad when an innocent person is killed, but The Powers That Be don't always intervene in every death—even every horrible, violent murder. They pick and choose their battles. So maybe the death of poor Mr. Barnett was a bad thing, but not a *bad* bad thing—which means, it's just a harbinger of a *bad* bad thing that's still on the way. There's a clue in it somewhere, or The Powers wouldn't have brought it to your attention, Cord. There must be worse things on the horizon, if we don't figure out the clue and act on it."

Angel nodded grimly. "That's pretty much the

same conclusion I came up with. On the face of it, we seem to be dealing with a stolen truckload of antiques. But since you haven't exactly been vision-girl lately, Cordy, I don't think you'd have been bothered with one now if there weren't something bigger going on. I just can't see what it is." He unfolded the photocopy he'd made of the bill of lading in the trucking office. "We'll have to do some research, figure out if there's something on this list that is more than it appears to be. I checked the destination address, and it's a state park—the Mission San Alejandro. The shipment came from a parks warehouse too, so that makes sense. Tomorrow we'll have to check that out."

"I can do that," Gunn volunteered.

At the same moment, Fred piped up, "I'll check the mission."

"Okay, Gunn and Fred, you two are on the mission. Cordy, you're on the computer, trying to run down the details of the stuff that was stolen."

"Got it, boss," Cordy said brightly. She sounded as if she'd never been away. "First thing in the morning."

Which reminded Angel that she wouldn't be spending the night here in the hotel, as she once would have. Rather, she would be spending it at whatever lodging Connor had come up with. He didn't know where that was but suspected it wasn't exactly the Ritz.

He couldn't really argue her point—they couldn't check out the mission park until it opened in the morning, and until they did that it seemed unlikely that they'd learn anything crucial. Anyway, there didn't seem to be any immediate urgency, now that the one victim they were aware of was already dead. So if she took off a few hours to get some shut-eye, what would it really hurt? His own inclination was always to charge into any situation right away. But Cordy was a higher being, or had been, and presumably had some of that higher being wisdom—and patience—going for her.

"Okay, let's get some rest," he said, knowing that he'd be out that night anyway. "First thing tomorrow we move on this."

"It was so exciting, Pookie," Mildred Finster told her cat. The creature's flat, bored expression didn't change, but he did give a soft purr that encouraged her to keep talking. "You should have seen me. The police officers just turned away Mr. Angel and his friend, but they fell all over themselves to help me."

Pookie stood on her lap and arched his back under her stroking fingers. "They told me everything I needed to know, and it was so easy. I don't think Miss Marple could have done it better. I really am a natural at this detecting thing."

She tickled the cat under his chin, and he closed

his eyes in contented bliss. "The body was worse than I imagined it could be," she continued with a shudder. "All that blood and . . . and other parts I can't even name . . . It looked as if whatever—whoever—had done that had torn the poor man's head off, as easily as I would tear a piece of paper. I wonder if I should have told Mr. Angel how brutal it was, so he would know just what kind of monster he's up against."

Seemingly in response Pookie licked one of his paws. "You're right," Mildred agreed. "I should have been more forceful about telling them what I saw. After all, they didn't get to see the body, and I did. They don't have any idea how bad it was. It might be a clue of some kind. Of course, I don't have any idea how they found out about it in the first place—certainly not from the police, since they found no cooperation there. I guess we all have some secrets from one another."

She lifted Pookie off her lap then, held the cat by the ribs, just behind his front legs, and looked him in the eye. "But after I solve this case, then they'll have to take me seriously, right? They can't turn me away if I prove that I'm good enough to join the firm, can they?"

The cat yawned, and seeing it set Mildred off into a yawn of her own. She put Pookie down on the carpet. "Oh, you're right again, Mr. P," she said. "It is late, and it's been a terribly eventful day.

ANGEL

And tomorrow will certainly be more so. If I'm going to get an early start, I'd better get off to bed now."

She went into the kitchen, checked his food dish, and made sure he had enough water to get through the night. Pookie was an indoor cat, not one of those toms who wandered the nighttime streets stirring up trouble and getting in fights, except for those times he escaped through an open door and went on his little instinctive hunting expeditions. But he was still nocturnal—and diurnal, in that he seemed to sleep away most of the day, every day. At night he was sentry and companion, roaming the house between naps and meal breaks, checking the windows and doors for his mistress. The house had been more than a little lonely since Philip had passed on, but Pookie had proven a brave and loyal companion, if a bit on the quiet side.

He took care of Mildred, and in return she took care of him. Seeing that he was in fine shape to survive the night, she kissed him once on the top of his furry head and went off to prepare for bed.

CHAPTER FOUR

The man who climbed down from the truck's high cab was dwarfed by the massive machine. He stood well under six feet, and though he kept his spine straight as he took crisp, efficient steps around the vehicle like a military commander inspecting his troops, his posture did not add significantly to his height. Nor was he a large man. His waist was slender, his hands and feet small, and in spite of his excellent posture his shoulders would never be described as broad.

He made a complete circuit of the big truck, examining wheels that were chest-high on him and bending over to peer at the undercarriage. The exterior was forest green, with CROSSWAYS FREIGHT printed in gigantic white letters across the long box of its trailer over a paler green outline of the state of California. There was other incidental lettering on the truck's surface, license information and so on, but none of that concerned him. When he had walked all the way around the truck, he took several steps back from it and regarded the whole thing as a single piece. He smoothed down his silver hair with one ringed hand, tugged at the cuffs of his fine silk suit, and then, composed and dignified in appearance, he stared at the vehicle as if willing it to give up its secrets. Anyone who happened to enter the seemingly abandoned warehouse on a crumbling, weed-choked cul-de-sac in Inglewood might believe the man had found himself there by accident: He looked old, sedate, and prosperous, not at all like the kind of man one would expect to see behind the wheel of an eighteen-wheeler or inside a run-down warehouse like this one.

But in fact, anyone who accidentally ran across this man in this place would find himself begging for his life within moments. For though this man, who was called Obregon, looked old, he was in fact far, far older than he appeared, and though he carried himself with dignity and grace, he had already killed three people today.

Which was nothing, really, compared with the last time he'd been in the neighborhood.

His external perusal of the truck completed, Obregon walked to the vehicle's rear. The cargo door was sealed by a heavy-duty padlock, but Obregon had taken the driver's key ring when he'd torn the fool's head off at the truck stop, and it took just moments to determine which of the many keys opened the lock. Obregon studied the lock for a moment, turning it this way and that in his hands, then tossed it into the warehouse's deep shadows. He shoved the truck's sliding door up. It rattled in its tracks but rolled into place, and Obregon climbed the bumper step into the trailer.

The truck had been carefully packed. At this end were several large cardboard cartons, sealed with tape and then shrink-wrapped onto pallets. Heavier items were closer to the trailer's front, strapped into place, with movers' blankets wrapped around them. What Obregon sought was very small, and could be anyplace, so he started with the boxes. He hooked the shrink-wrap with rigid fingers and shredded it like cotton candy, tossing it to the floor of the warehouse as he did. Rather than cut the tape, he just drove his fingers through the cardboard and tore it away, revealing the contents of each carton.

The first contained small silver pieces, each individually wrapped in plastic. Candle holders, small crosses, bells, cups—as he hurled them across the warehouse they bounced and clattered like chimes in a hurricane wind. The next box, even more carefully wrapped, contained gold objects that met the same fate. Obregon worked quickly through the boxes, his anger starting to build as each one proved not to contain the object of his search.

By the time he had finished with the cartons, Obregon's face was red and his hands were quaking slightly with rage. The big items remained, and what he sought could have been hidden among them, though it would have made more sense to simply pack it in a box with the other things of approximately equal size. He snapped one of the heavy webbed nylon straps holding a church pew in place and dragged the pew into the section of truck he'd already emptied, scattering shreds of cardboard and plastic wrap before it. Kneeling on the pew, he checked its joints, but it seemed securely put together, even after all these years. He looked behind it and underneath it. No hidey-holes or secret compartments were visible. Squatting slightly, he gripped the bench and back and lifted it into the air, shaking it and listening for unex-pected sounds. The old wood groaned but there was nothing else. Veins in his neck stood out slightly at this effort, but lifting the heavy pew barely strained his abilities.

Replacing it on the truck trailer's floor, he went to the far end of it and grabbed the armrest. He wrenched on it a couple of times until the wood gave way and separated from the pew. The bench thudded to the floor. Obregon inspected the armrest carefully, then tossed it into the far shadows.

He returned to the rest of the pew and tore it apart, section by section, with his bare hands. As with the boxes before, each part was thrown aside when it was revealed not to hide the object he wanted.

He repeated the process with everything else in the truck. Marble statues were crumbled to dust in his hands. He ripped the gold filigree from an ornate altar before dismantling the structure piece by piece. He peeled apart the layers of iron that composed an enormous bell. But even that held no secrets for him.

Finally the truck was empty and the warehouse floor was a sea of refuse. The man who had met Obregon here early in the day, believing he had come to show the warehouse to a prospective tenant, would have been horrified at the condition if he hadn't been back in the shadows himself, lying in a pool of his own blood and guts, his chest cracked open like a walnut by Obregon's powerful hands.

Still, the truck had refused to divulge the secret Obregon believed it hid. His anger now a red rage, Obregon turned to the vehicle itself. He started inside it, forcing his hands through the bed's metal floor and peeling it up in long strips. When there was nothing left to stand on he took to the walls, tearing them apart. He ripped the giant tires from the wheels and shredded them like tissue paper, scattering rubber everywhere. He tore apart the engine, then the cab, destroying the seats and sleeping compartment, wrecking the instruments, and even breaking through the paneling to look inside the roof and doors.

At the end of it Obregon's silver hair was mussed and hanging in his eyes, his hands bloody and torn, his once-fine suit now filthy and shredded. But that didn't matter; there were always more nice suits to be had. Obregon's first victim of the day, before the warehouse owner and the truck driver, had been a salesman in a clothing boutique in West Hollywood. There were plenty more boutiques to visit, though; the gigantic metropolis that Los Angeles had become in his long absence was crawling with them.

The truck itself was barely identifiable. Moving through the warehouse was like wading in a knee-high sea of debris, much of it metal and sharp-edged. And still Obregon didn't have what he wanted most in the world.

He went to the warehouse's smaller door, the human-size one, and opened it, looking out at the empty nighttime street, its one light burning over a patch of weeds and some broken concrete. It was still out there, then. Somewhere in Los Angeles, he was certain. He *would* find it—the city would no more keep its secrets from him than the truck had.

And anyone who got in his way would live just long enough to regret his mistake.

"Are you sure you don't want me to stay longer, Wes?" Lilah Morgan purred. She stood at the door, leaning her head against its edge, hands sensuously caressing the wood near her face. Her eyes were half-closed in an imitation of lust and she flicked her tongue across her lips. At once repelled and attracted, Wesley Wyndam-Pryce had to look away lest the attraction win out again.

"Quite sure, Lilah," he managed. He was expecting another visitor, one he didn't want Lilah to meet. Not because he didn't want Lilah to know, but because, as unsavory as his late night assignation would be, he would still be ashamed for his visitor to see Lilah here. Like an avalanche in a mountain pass, she was beautiful and deadly at the same time. Wesley thought the instinct that kept drawing him back to her was the same that caused a motorist to slow down to look at a bloody roadside accident—some perverse circular combination of disgust and curiosity. It was even stronger in this case because he truly desired Lilah, even though he suspected that it was mostly because he wanted to punish himself, because turning to Lilah shamed him as he felt he deserved. He had betrayed Angel, betrayed his best friends, and for that he felt a self-loathing that being with Lilah reinforced.

"Go," he said forcefully. "Get out of here."

"If you're absolutely certain," Lilah said, making no effort to leave. "Because I don't have anyplace better to be or anything—anyone—better to do."

"Lilah," Wesley said, his voice heavy with warning. "Now."

"Until next time, then. And there *will* be a next time. You know there will." She slipped out the door and closed it gently behind her. Wes felt his guts churn as she left. He didn't want her to go, already missed her, in fact. But at the same time he always felt cleaner when she had gone. Resolve built inside him. *I'll never see her again, never invite her back here,* he told himself. But he told himself that every time. And every time, he failed; his good intentions gave way to his weak will, and he called her or went to her.

She knew what the game was. She acted docile, submissive to his will, but she was playing him and they both knew it. Wes stood there, alone in his own apartment, looking at the door she had just touched, and felt his emotions crash against themselves like waves pulling back from the beach, caught up in more powerful ones pushing forward.

He had stolen Angel's son, sided with Angel's enemies, been betrayed in turn by them, and had his throat cut. He had survived, and had even rescued Angel from exile at sea. But there had been no forgiveness for his crimes, either from Angel or within himself. Each day he spent away from his former teammates was punishment, and as day grew into night—the time when, before, he'd have been on the prowl with them, battling evil side by side with the bravest people he'd ever known—his self-hatred grew, his will weakened, and he found himself reaching out to Lilah, who only confirmed every bad thing he believed about himself.

Wesley was caught in a vicious cycle of self-recrimination and self-defeating punishment. The more he saw Lilah, the more he hated himself for seeing her. The more he hated himself, the more he was driven to punish himself by seeing her again. He was fully aware of this pattern. He wanted nothing on earth more than to break out of it.

But wanting it and doing it were two very different things. It was easy to want. Sometimes it was easy to have what he wanted—as when he wanted Lilah. Other times it seemed impossible. He wanted to end this cycle, to restore himself to Angel's good graces, to be loved by Fred. But Fred loved Gunn, and therein lay another of many insurmountable obstacles. Fred loved Gunn and Angel hated Wes. Until those two things changed—which seemed unlikely in the extreme—Wes believed he would be stuck where he was, tormenting himself with Lilah, hunting alone at night to salve what conscience he had left.

Of course, there was one other possibility—one that nagged at him from time to time, though he was usually successful in pushing it back into the farthest recesses of his mind. *What if I'm starting to care for her?* he thought.

No! That wasn't possible. It didn't even bear giving serious thought to—

A knock at the door startled him from his reverie. *Lilah again?* No, she wouldn't come back until he begged her to. He pulled open the door.

"Hello, Wesley." It was Franz, whose last name Wesley had never known, or asked. All Wes knew about him was that he worked with Emil and spoke with an indeterminate central European accent. Franz had a thick shock of black hair and a scar that started somewhere above the hairline, bisected his milky white and sightless right eye, and ended at the corner of his mouth, which it tugged into a false smile. In his left fist Franz held a black cloth gym bag.

"Come in, Franz," Wesley said quickly, glad that Lilah was gone. He stepped aside as Franz entered, the bag in his hand jingling slightly. "You have what I ordered?"

"If you have the price," Franz said. His body was compact and solid; arm muscles stretched his tight shirtsleeves to their limit. He made a good delivery person—anyone would think twice about trying to relieve him of merchandise without paying first.

"Set it down there," Wesley instructed, pointing to a dining room table half-obscured under books and papers. When he ate at home these days, he did so in the kitchen, standing at the counter. He had once appreciated fine food, but now dining was a necessity, not a pleasure, and he put the least effort possible into it.

Franz did as he was told, setting the bag on the table and unzipping it. While he did so, Wesley took an envelope from its perch across the top of some books on one of his bookshelves and thumbed open the flap. The agreed-on price was inside, with no bills larger than twenties, as Emil had specified. Wesley carried it to the table.

Franz looked at the envelope, then up at Wesley's face, his own marred visage breaking into what seemed to be a genuine smile, no less frightening for its honesty than his usual scar-created one. "Very good," he said. His *v* had a soft *f* quality to it, and he ended the second word with a hard *t* sound, so his sentence came out as "fery goot." He said it a second time as he took the envelope from Wesley's hand, tucked it into a jeans pocket, and began to remove items from the bag. "Very good."

"A dagger," he said as he drew it out. "Silver, of course. Runic protections on its blade. Tempered, both edges sharpened, dipped twice in human blood. A leather scabbard that fastens around your ankle."

"Excellent," Wesley replied. *Just as Emil described it,* he thought. He took the dagger from Franz and felt its comfortable heft. Its pommel was wrapped in soft leather and the silver hand guard kept it perfectly balanced. "What else?"

Franz reached into the bag again and brought out a roll of leather. Holding one end, he released the other, and the strip spooled out to reveal a series of identical wooden stakes, sharpened to fine points. "Ironwood," Franz told him.

Strongest wood on the planet, Wes knew. *Hence the name.* These were stakes that would not shatter or splinter easily. Franz held the leather strap diagonally across his own barrel chest. "You wear it this way, like a bandolier," he explained. "Under a coat, perhaps. All the stakes are in easy reach."

"Very good," Wesley said with a smile, unconsciously mimicking Franz's own phrase. "What about the other thing?"

"The spring-loads?" Franz asked. "Emil needs more time for those. A bit more."

Wesley realized his error in handing over the envelope, which was already in Franz's pocket. "Then I shouldn't pay the full amount yet."

Franz inhaled with a huff, swelling out his already huge chest. "You don't trust?" he demanded. "You trust Emil, you trust me. We always live up to promises."

That much is true, Wesley thought. Since he'd

been doing business with Emil he hadn't been disappointed or cheated. Which was more than he could say for some other suppliers he'd dealt with, fly-by-night dealers who'd use their weapons on an unsuspecting client, then keep both weapons and money. But Emil had always come through for him, and his weaponry was top quality. When he delivered on an enchanted object, it truly was enchanted, and with the correct spells and materials, which was important.

"Very well," Wesley said finally. "Keep the payment. Just be sure that Emil comes through." He had ordered spring-loaded blades that could go up his sleeves, to be shot out into his hands when he needed them. He figured that Franz was being honest—the mechanics of the spring-loading would require more time and effort than these simpler weapons.

Franz ticked his finger back and forth like a metronome. "Don't worry," he assured Wesley as he zipped the big bag. "Everything will be fine. Just like you order. Maybe tomorrow, maybe next day."

"The sooner the better," Wesley told him. Franz lifted the now-empty bag easily and made for the door. He tossed Wesley another ghastly smile and was gone. Wes pulled the dagger from its sheath and looked at the blade. But it was too shiny—he could see himself reflected in it, and he was grizzled and unkempt, hair still mussed from Lilah's visit. He didn't like what he saw, so he jammed it back into the scabbard and threw it down on the table.

Madelyn Kinross had trouble sleeping, most nights. She could take a sleeping pill or two, but they knocked her out so deeply that nothing could rouse her, and she worried about Gene when she did that. So instead she drank a little warm milk or some herbal tea shortly before bed, and tried to empty her mind of the day's troubles with a romance novel or some mindless TV. It was hard, though; she was always worried: about Gene, about making ends meet and keeping up the mortgage payments on the house, about hanging on to her job, and whatever other cares the day presented. She was gaunt now—she had worried herself down to ninety-eight pounds from a healthier one-twenty over the past decades—and her auburn hair had gone mostly white.

This particular night she had turned out the lights at eleven, then had stayed in bed, tossing and rolling and clawing for sleep, until about twelve-thirty. Her dreams had been stressful almost from the start—creatures chasing her down empty streets and dark hallways, presences looming around her in the shadows. But they had been interrupted, barely an hour into her much-needed sleep, by the first noise of the night.

Madelyn tried to ignore it, and at first her dreams played along, incorporating the distant thump. But then there was another one, and another, and gradually she roused from sleep, knowing that it was not part of a dream but solid, and hated, reality. By the time she swung her legs around and found her footing, the sounds had become louder and closer together. At first she had thought that maybe it was someone in the house. It sounded like a rainstorm now, rain and thunder all in one, continuous and unrelenting. But she knew that wasn't it. Nothing so simple, of course, not for the Kinross household.

Madelyn was torn between terror and rage—anger at whatever forces had picked her, out of all the beings in the universe, to torment so, and terror because whatever force it was, she knew that it was more powerful than could be believed. Nothing natural could do the things it did. Nor would any beneficent force target her in this way, she was convinced. No, this was evil, no other way to look at it.

She shook cobwebs of sleep from her mind and headed for Gene's room, as she always did when an event like this happened. There hadn't been so terribly many of them over the decades—a few dozen, maybe, but they stuck in her mind when they occurred. There had been the time that a tree crashed through the window of Gene's room—

even though the land around their place had been cleared for thirty yards, to keep fire danger down. And when she had gone out the next day to look, there hadn't been any trees missing from the surrounding forest, so it wasn't like one had run over to the house, or been thrown there by a freak tornado that had mysteriously left the rest of the neighborhood untouched. On another occasion doors and windows that had been locked and bolted had opened up and starting slamming open and closed, as if in a monstrous windstorm. But there had been no wind at all.

It had been like that, over the years. Inexplicable happenings. Invasions of her home, her spirit, her soul. She had sought out "experts," but few had believed her and none had been able to help her. The ones who were most interested in trying tended to be people she wasn't comfortable inviting into her home anyway. So she just lived with the horror, hoping every night as she drifted off that tonight she would be spared.

Now, as she always did, she looked in on Gene, hoping that the thunderous racket wasn't disturbing him—but some part of her, at the same time, wishing it would. As usual, he was totally oblivious to the deafening clatter and roar. Gene Kinross had been comatose since 1973. Like the events that plagued their household, no expert had been able to explain the nature of his coma, or how he had managed to live, without even visibly aging, for all these years. Her husband looked as he always did, like he had thirty years ago, sleeping a deep, restful sleep. The mad drummer pounding on their roof didn't phase him.

Madelyn went to the window of his room and looked out. Rocks—some small, barely pebbles, others the size of softballs or grapefruit—rained down on the roof with such a horrific racket, then rolled to the ground. There was already a growing pile down there that she could see in the light that spilled out through Gene's window, like snow drifting against the house. The rain continued until she was certain it would tear through the roof and crush her at any moment.

But then, as suddenly as it had started, it stopped. A few last rocks fell, then just one by itself, and then it was over. Madelyn had tears running down her cheeks, and she clutched Gene's lifeless hand in both of hers, held it to her face, and she wondered why.

CHAPTER FIVE

Fred sat in nervous silence as close to the door of the truck as she could get. She had been uncomfortable around Charles Gunn ever since that—that incident, which she could barely bring herself to think about. It had tainted the way she felt about Charles, and she wasn't quite sure how she would ever get past that. So when the two of them had been dispatched to the Mission San Alejandro together, she had been hesitant. But she always tried to do what Angel asked. He had saved her life, more times now than she could actually keep track of. He had brought her home, back to Earth, after her nightmare time in Pylea. So she swallowed her concerns and went with Charles, the man she had so recently loved. She still did, she thought, love him, in some of the definitions of that word. But she also couldn't help fearing him a little bit.

This was not a healthy combination. So instead of yakking good naturedly the way she ordinarily would have—even if only out of nervous tension—she found herself with nothing at all to say. She recognized that this was an extraordinarily rare occurrence, but it seemed beyond her control. Every now and then Charles tried to pry conversation from her, but his attempts were as subtle as a crowbar and easily evaded.

"Look at that big boat," he said once, pointing out a monstrous SUV that looked as if it could have carried an entire football team across the Sahara. "Must use a gallon of gas every mile just to keep going."

"Yeah, I guess," was all Fred could say in reply.

A little while later Charles tried again. "Sky sure is blue today. Good thing we're the ones going to the mission instead of Angel—gonna be a sunny one."

"Good thing," Fred managed.

Mercifully the drive to Chino was unencumbered by any southern California traffic jams, so before Fred actually melted into her seat, they started up the mission park's driveway, a modern paved road that led up a steep, grassy slope outside of town. At the top of the drive they found a large parking lot with just a few other vehicles in it. Charles parked the truck and they both got out, blinking in the sunlight.

A flagstone walkway led away from the parking lot through a lush, trellised garden overgrown with bright violet bougainvillea and other colorful flowers. Rising above the garden on the other side was a whitewashed wall that gleamed in the sun's rays. Fred could see a doorway set into the wall, a window up above the door, and some ornamentation around them, though most of it was obscured by the thick foliage. To the right of the door the wall rose up even higher than it did above the window and made a kind of scalloped arch, and inset into holes cut away from the wall were two bells. Two other holes gaped vacantly, their massive bells missing.

"Didn't Angel say there were some bells on the stolen truck?" Fred asked, pointing out the empty spots. "Maybe they go there."

"Looks like," Charles agreed. "Be some big bells, though."

"Let's go in," she suggested, heading for the walkway without waiting for his answer. On the way in she passed a large wooden sign reading MISSION SAN ALEJANDRO: A CALIFORNIA STATE PARK. There was a little container of paper park guides attached to the signpost, so she helped herself to one.

The mission's massive door—three inches of solid wood, carved in an ornate fashion—stood open, offering entrance to a shaded walkway. The adobe wall itself was at least a foot thick, Fred noted. She glanced back to see that Charles was following, but slowly, looking around as if he expected an ambush at any point. Fred shrugged and kept going, passing through the enormous doorway into the mission's interior. A rope and stanchion passageway led to a gift shop, in which uniformed park employees sold day passes to the mission grounds, as well as books, postcards, posters, and other souvenirs.

Fred dug into her pocket and came up with enough cash to buy two passes. She pointed to Charles, who was still outside the shop looking at the grounds over the ropes. "The other one's for him," she said. "He's kind of with me."

"That's fine," the woman behind the counter said. "You both have a nice visit, okay?"

"I'm sure we will," Fred promised her.

Finally Charles caught up and they went through another door of the gift shop and onto the mission grounds proper. The gift shop was built into the largest structure, which had a wooden cross on top and narrow windows cut high into the sides. The guide Fred had picked up identified it as the chapel. It was set into the right front corner of a large quadrangle, which surrounded a vast open square that must have been two hundred feet across. According to the guide, the shaded walkway ringed the interior walls of the quadrangle, facing onto the square. The various other rooms were off this main walkway. Like the rest of the place, its walls were whitewashed adobe, topped with red tile roofs.

The square itself had a fountain in its center with a large statue of Father Junipero Serra as its focal point. Father Serra, Fred knew, had been the first Spanish padre to come to the state specifically to found the chain of missions that stretched from San Diego up the coast into northern California. In this statue he stood peacefully, arms casually crossed over his chest, with a beatific look on his face as he gazed over his handiwork. Gardens surrounded the statue, and nearby was a shade *ramada* with picnic tables underneath it. A beehive-looking structure about three feet tall was identified by Fred's park guide as an *hornito*, or clay oven. A few tourists strolled across the grounds or followed the self-guided tour, and Fred saw a park ranger in a Smokey hat answering questions.

"It's pretty," Fred said. She still felt apprehensive about being alone with Charles, but it helped to have a task to think about.

"That's great," Charles said. "But it don't help us any."

"Do you have any suggestions?" Fred said.

Charles inclined his head toward the ranger. "Let's get him alone and talk to him."

Without a better alternative to suggest, Fred agreed. They waited until he was finished talking to a small clutch of tourists and had started walking in their direction, across the plaza. Then they emerged from the shade, back into bright sunlight, and intersected his path.

"Sir, I wonder, could we talk to you? Just for a few minutes?" Fred said when they reached him.

The ranger looked them both up and down. She thought that perhaps they didn't look quite like the typical tourists. She clutched the park guide in one hand, but they didn't have cameras or guidebooks or even the sun visors that so many of the tourists she saw, unused to California's golden weather, wore everywhere they went. But he was smiling when he replied. "Sure. What can I do you for?"

Charles spoke first, and Fred didn't mind deferring to him in this instance. "We know there was a truck headed here that was stolen yesterday," he said bluntly. "We were wondering what you could tell us about it."

The ranger's eyes narrowed. "And your interest is . . . ?"

"We're private investigators," Charles told him. "Crossways Freight . . ." He didn't go so far as to tell the lie Fred was afraid he might, just left the name of the trucking company hanging in the air.

But the ranger bought into it. "I can see why

ANGEL

they'd be concerned. Bad business all the way around."

"Yes, sir," Fred said. "Very bad. Bad, bad, bad business." Deciding she had thrown a few too many "bads" out there, she closed her mouth.

"The truck?" Charles prompted.

"There's not really that much I can tell you," the ranger said. "The State Parks Department is closing a warehouse up north—budgetary reasons. Lucky they're closing warehouses instead of parks, I suppose. Various mission artifacts had been stored there for a long time—decades, I guess—while we did some substantial reconstruction and restoration to the mission grounds. Restoration is still ongoing, but with the warehouse closing, the furnishings and artifacts were being returned here. We were going to put them in storage on our grounds until we were ready for them. That's what was on the truck."

"And you don't have any idea who would want to intercept that shipment?"

"Not a clue," the ranger answered. "Some of it is valuable enough, I guess. But it'd be hard to sell. Legitimate antique dealers would know it had been stolen and wouldn't touch it. And somehow I don't think most pawn shops or fences deal in these kinds of items."

"Probably not," Charles said with a wry smile.

"I'd help you more if I could," the ranger assured them. "I hope you find the truck, and I'm really sorry about the driver. But I just don't have a thing to go on."

"That's okay, sir," Fred said sympathetically. "Thank you for your help."

After the ranger had gone on his way, Charles snorted softly. "Help?" he echoed. "What help?"

"He told us what he knew," Fred pointed out.

"Which is nothing."

"We know more than we did before," Fred said. "We know why there was a truck full of the mission's things out there."

"Which does absolutely nothing for us," Charles insisted. "We already knew what was in the truck. Knowing why doesn't make things any clearer unless we also knew that someone didn't want that stuff delivered to the mission, for whatever reason. Or someone wanted something that was on the truck."

Fred looked at the dirt floor of the plaza. "I guess you're right," she said with some reluctance. Normally when he was acting this way, discouraged or negative, she could cajole him out of it. Or smooch him out of it.

But today, she thought, *neither of those options is going to happen.*

Mildred Finster stood behind a stone column on the shadowed walkway, straining to hear what Gunn and Fred were saying. Apparently they had learned the contents of the truck, which had put them one up on her. But she'd been able to hear the ranger clearly—he had been facing in her direction and was used to projecting his voice for tour groups. In the midmorning quiet, his words had been quite distinct.

So now it seemed she was back on the same page that they were. As Mr. Gunn had said, it didn't help to know what the cargo was unless one also knew who had an interest in that cargo. On that score Angel Investigations was every bit as in the dark as Finster Investigations.

Now she noticed that Fred and Gunn had turned around and were headed back toward the walkway. It wouldn't do to be seen here, so she hurried farther down the walkway, away from the big chapel building, and turned into the first open doorway she saw. It led to restored living quarters for the padres who had established the mission in 1773, according to an explanatory sign on the wall. Their furnishings had been primitive—beds composed of rough hewn logs with leather straps crisscrossing between them, a primitive kneeling chair, a crucifix on the wall, and a couple of old trunks for their clothing and personal items. She knew enough history to know that the padres hadn't come here to get rich, and that, although the missions themselves sometimes generated good income through farming and small-scale industry, that income went back to Spain or the Church, not to the clerics themselves. She looked around the room for a few minutes, getting a sense of how hard life must have been for these men. They had come in pairs, for the most part, because they didn't consider the Indians they came to live among—or the soldiers who accompanied them—as capable of having complex intellectual conversation. More than one padre, alone for too long, had gone insane over the years.

Mildred went back to the big doorway and peeked outside. She saw Fred and Gunn heading into the gift shop, presumably on their way back to the parking lot. Feeling secure, she stepped back onto the walkway and continued her search.

They were giving up too easily, she thought. One ranger hadn't been able to help them, and maybe none of the others would either. But the answer—part of the answer, at least—had to be here. Unless the truck had been chosen entirely at random, this mission played a part in the puzzle. And she had seen the violence done to the truck driver. To her, that didn't look like a random act.

She made her way along the walkway, glad for the protection its arched cover gave from the sun. She passed storerooms, a workshop, and living quarters for Indians who had worked at the mission, which were far more cramped and spartan than even the padres' room had been. At the far end of the quadrangle, away from the chapel, the buildings were in worse repair. There the whitewash was black with age and mildew, the red roof tiles broken and missing. Doors were closed and locked, or sealed off with yellow caution tape. Through an open passageway that was also blocked by the yellow tape she could see yet more buildings off to one side of the main quadrangle, and by leaning her head out and craning it she spotted a small cemetery enclosed by a wrought iron fence. These were both contained within a separate, lower adobe wall that encircled grounds that must once have been used for farming.

There were no tourists at this end of the plaza, as if they somehow knew there was nothing here for them. Mildred had heard the ranger talking about the restoration efforts, and this was probably the section he had mentioned that wasn't yet finished. Which meant, of course, that it was the ultimate destination of most of the items on the truck. This area was quiet; the hushed, distant voices of tourists on the square sounded no more distinct than the whispering of leaves in a soft summer breeze. She took a quick look around to make sure no one was watching her, and then slipped under the yellow tape and hurried down the short breezeway.

A moment later she broke free of the main quadrangle and followed the well-worn dirt path to the first of the three outbuildings. Like the back corner, the whitewash here had seen better days. *Or better centuries,* she thought. The roof had caved in and been patched with plastic sheeting, in preparation, she guessed, for being rebuilt altogether. The building had a few windows, open rectangles behind iron bars, and a heavy wooden door with a crossbar closure. Something seemed strange about that, but Mildred had to look at it for a couple of minutes before she realized that it would have made more sense—or been more traditional, at least—for the crossbar to be on the inside of the building, and not the outside.

The other buildings were the same way: long, narrow, low-ceilinged, and in serious disrepair. There were "closed for repair" signs on all the doors, and she had a feeling—well, she knew, given that she'd already broken the rule by sneaking beneath the tape—that she wasn't supposed to be out there.

If she had been hoping these buildings would speak to her, she was disappointed. They stood mute, closed off to her and the rest of the world. After she made a complete loop around them she gave up for the moment and went back to the passageway into the quadrangle. When she arrived there, she ducked under the tape again and struck out across the sunny plaza for the exit and her car.

Through the bars Graham Taylor watched the old woman's departing form with a sense of relief. She was likely just a busybody, one of those people who thought signs were there for everyone else's benefit but not for theirs. She certainly didn't look like a threat, and he wouldn't even bother to report her presence. *Don't make trouble where it doesn't have to be made,* that was his philosophy. *Why stir things up?* If he'd been the kind of guy who sought out ways to make life difficult, he'd have taken a straight job, selling shoes or something. But that life didn't agree with him. He needed some variety in his days, and he liked to do the least possible work for the greatest possible reward. This situation, he knew, was likely to get complicated enough on its own; he didn't need to muck it up any further with tales of nosy old ladies poking around.

If she'd been more persistent, of course, he'd have had to deal with her, like it or not. And he'd been prepared to. That was why he'd been given this assignment, after all, because he was a fellow who could be counted on when things went south. He double-checked the Glock before replacing it in the holster that hung at his armpit, to make sure the safety was on. Then he turned back to the inside door, the one set into the floor that led to a flight of stairs, narrow and worn smooth with the passing of time and many, many sandaled feet. Another crisis averted, at least for now.

He was always glad of that.

A wind rustled the palm fronds outside his study, but far more insistent was the sound of drums that he had heard all morning. Obregon stood by the window, breathing in the fresh air. A few workers toiled in the garden outside, backs bent to their tasks. He tried to ignore their near nakedness as he called one over. "You there!" he shouted. They all looked up at him, so he crooked his finger at one. They had learned that was a summoning, though it had taken some a few beatings to get it straight.

That one glanced at his fellows and then approached the window. "What is that noise?" Obregon asked. "That drumming? It's been going on all morning."

The worker looked confused. No surprise, that—he was simple, as they all were, and needed the lash and the Lord to set him right. He was a lamb of the flock, and Obregon needed to exercise patience with all of them. "The drums!" Obregon clarified.

"Drums," the worker repeated. "Magick. Many magick."

Obregon sniffed in surprise. He knew they had been learning Spanish, but he didn't know the word for magick was part of the vocabulary lessons. Miracle, certainly. But magick? He would have to have a talk with Padre Escamilla about that. "The drums are magick?"

The worker smiled at him. "Yes," he said. "Big magick."

Obregon turned away from the window, dismissing the innocent wordlessly. It makes sense, *he supposed,* that these primitives have their own magicks. Primitive peoples always have. *He had, before the infernal drumming had disturbed him, been studying a text that described magickal rituals of the ancient Britons, particularly some of the Highland and isle-dwelling peoples whose crops, in those forbidding climes, required a good bit of supernatural assistance.*

Obregon had never been one to believe that the Lord's magick was all there was, all that worked on this Earth. It was the cleanest, of course, and the safest. But safety was not his overriding concern. Power was. And if there was a way to combine these primitive native magicks with the European traditions he had already studied so carefully, he might be able to amass a great deal of it.

He resolved at that moment to get his hands on one of their magicians and see what he could learn. It could be profitable, *he believed.* Very profitable indeed.

CHAPTER SIX

Angel found Cordelia at the computer when he came downstairs. "Get enough sleep?" he asked her, for lack of anything better to say. Or anything he thought she'd want to hear, at any rate. He could think of plenty to say, but not much that would be welcomed right now.

She turned away from the monitor and favored him with a smile that cut like a dagger. "Well, you know," she said. "'Enough sleep' isn't really part of my vocabulary anymore. But I'm functional, if that's what you mean."

"I guess that has to be good enough," he replied.

"I remember back in high school—and it's nice to be able to remember, I can tell you that—there were days that I slept for fourteen hours or more and didn't feel like I'd had enough. Usually after a late night, of course. I thought people slowed down as they got older, needed more sleep, but if I got any more than that I would have been extinct, I guess."

"You may be a special case," Angel suggested. "Having been a higher being, and all that."

"I think that's part of it," she agreed, swiveling her chair around to face him. "I don't seem to need as much sleep as I did before. And I can go longer without hunger pains, you know, pokin' at me. But it was before that too. I mean, our schedule, come on. Up in the daytime researching evil or fighting it, up at night fighting evil some more. Doesn't leave a lot of time for beauty rest."

Not that you need it, he thought. Cordy looked as good as she ever did, or better, fresh-faced and alive. The higher being thing had agreed with her, there was no doubt about that. He couldn't help wishing that she was suffering just a little, that maybe Connor's place was exceedingly noisy or uncomfortable, so she'd reconsider and start sleeping at the hotel again. Or that, along with her other regained memories, she would remember how she had felt about him and would allow herself to feel that again.

She turned back toward the computer. "Anyway," she said over her shoulder, yanking the conversation back to business, "I've been looking up the items on that bill of lading you found. There's not much information online about most of them—they were kind of standard-issue mission junk from the late 1700s. Valuable, I guess, but nothing special for what they were. But there are a few scholars of that period who have written about Mission San Alejandro, and that's what I'm wading through now."

Angel regarded her back for a moment, the way her hair curled in toward her neck. . . . He forced himself to look away. Pining over Cordy wasn't going to help anything. She'd come around, when the time was right.

Or not.

"I'm . . . going to go read," he said, suddenly feeling an urgent need to get away from her, bury himself in some other task. "Some books. Wes's old books. See what I can find out in them."

"Good idea," Cordy answered distractedly, already immersed in her own research again.

Angel went to one of the shelves where Wes stored some of his many magickal tomes. Angel wasn't even sure they were dealing with magick, though—the truck driver's death and the theft of the vehicle could have been plain old human nastiness. What he needed, he guessed, was a mystical history of the mission era that might give him some kind of clue as to what in a shipment of items to Mission San Alejandro might attract the attention of The Powers That Be. What he *really* needed was something to punch, but there were no handy targets presenting themselves right now.

He was still perusing the shelves when Lorne breezed into the room. "You're bright-eyed and bushy-tailed this morning," the demon said cheerfully. "Getting an early start on the eternal struggle?"

"Rust never sleeps," Angel shot back. "Neither does evil."

"If only we had spray cans of Evil-Oleum people could squirt on it when it comes around, you could retire," Lorne said. "Find yourself a nice dark cave someplace tropical and take long nighttime walks on the beach."

"It's never that simple, is it?" Angel asked wearily.

"Nothing is," Lorne said. "'Simple' is a concept that's vastly exaggerated. Like those magazines that tell you how to live a simple life by spending a small fortune with their advertisers." Lorne cocked his head to one side and fixed Angel with his red eyes. "But you weren't talking about that, were you?"

Angel chuckled. "What, I don't even have to sing now?"

"Honey," Lorne said, "people only need to sing to let me look beneath the surface. You're an open book."

"Open to *you*," Angel countered. "Not everyone seems able to read me so easily."

"Some people are emotionally dyslexic," Lorne

opined. "Others wear blinders by choice. And some are just not ready to open their eyes yet, like newborn puppies."

"Which one is—never mind."

Lorne mimed pulling a zipper across his lips. "Not minding here, boss," he said. "I've got no problem talking to you about you, Angel. When it comes to giving up other people's secrets, sometimes I have to draw the line. Even if those secrets are about you."

"So you *do* know secrets about me?"

"I didn't say that. Look, tall, dark, and pushy, you're the one who said 'never mind.' I'm just taking you at your word."

"I know, Lorne," Angel said, resigning himself to continuing in ignorance of Cordelia's true feelings. If she had any at all. "Thanks anyway."

"If I knew what you were thanking me for," Lorne said, "you'd be most welcome, I'm sure."

Gunn tapped his fingers against the steering wheel, drumming along to a song in his head. Coolio's "Gangsta's Paradise." Music had once been important to him, but in these last few years—since the twin deaths of his sister Alonna, really, first at the hands of a vampire and then at his own hands, when he had to stake her to keep her from existing as one of the undead—music had taken a backseat, along with nearly everything else in life, to combat. To the eternal struggle of good versus evil.

He wasn't even sure he could name a top ten song these days. His life had been so completely overwhelmed by the fight that he just hadn't paid much attention to the world outside. Somehow Cordelia stayed on top of things—she made jokes about current TV shows that he'd never seen or heard of, commented on topical books, followed fashion. And Lorne seemed to know everything about music. Gunn felt like he'd been living with his head in a bag.

But there was one spark, one glowing ember that had brought him out from inside that bag. For a while he had fought simply because that was all he knew, all he remembered. The battle gave him a reason to be, to keep going. But now that he'd fallen in love with Fred, he fought because he wanted to keep her safe—wanted to keep the world safe for others like her, and for innocents everywhere. *Young lovers should be able to hold hands in the moonlight without worrying that some bloodsucker's going to chomp on them,* he thought. *Even if they're not me.*

But now that had gone bad somehow. They sat together in the truck outside the mission, but instead of talking and sharing and laughing, or making out, as they once might have done, there was a stilted, uncomfortable silence like an unwelcome and slightly smelly older relative sitting between them. Heading back to the truck after their brief reconnaissance trip, Fred had spotted a very familiar-looking red Dodge Dart in the lot. "Isn't that Mildred Finster's car?" she asked. "I saw her get out of it last night at the truck stop."

Gunn swore. "That lady followed us again? She's better at this than we are."

"Not quite," Fred argued. "If she was she wouldn't have parked where we'd be sure to spot her when we came out."

"I guess that's true," Gunn said, laughing. "Think we should leave her a note?"

"I think we should wait for her," Fred said, suddenly turning serious. "This could be dangerous, Charles. She might not understand that. We need to make her understand."

"But what if it's not her car?" Gunn wanted to know. "Or what if she just happened to come here as a tourist, because she heard the mission mentioned last night and wanted to check it out?"

"We didn't even know about the mission until Angel broke into the trucking company's office," Fred reminded him. "Not at the truck stop. She *had* to have followed us here."

"All right, then," Gunn said. "I guess we wait."

And wait they did. Finally, almost forty minutes after they had left the mission, Mildred Finster emerged. She wore a blouse with a paisley pattern, a pink skirt, and what Gunn had always heard referred to as "sensible shoes." *Granny shoes, more like,* he thought. Gunn and Fred shared a glance and got out of the truck at the same time, hurrying to reach the woman's car before she did.

Mildred was walking with her head down, as if watching for dropped coins, Gunn thought, or maybe just lost in thought. But when she reached her car she looked up, saw him and Fred, and broke into a startled smile. "Oh, it's you," she said. Not at all convincingly, she followed with, "Are you going to tour the mission? It's lovely."

"We've been," Gunn said flatly. "As you know."

"As I . . ." She stopped, giving up the innocent act. *For the best,* Gunn thought. She kind of reminded him of his grandma, who in turn had always reminded him of Jessica Fletcher, the old lady detective on TV, except that his grandma wasn't so pale and squeaky. So maybe there was something to his stream-of-consciousness connections, and Mildred really was meant to be a detective. His grandma had been curious and bulldog tenacious too, making it almost impossible to hide anything from her. "I did pretty well, didn't I?"

"You should have parked in a better place," Fred offered.

Mildred waved a hand around the mostly-empty lot. "I did think about that, but there are so few cars here you could have seen it anywhere. And I didn't want to walk for half a mile to get here. So I just hoped you wouldn't remember what I drove."

"That's a lot of hopin' for a detective," Gunn pointed out. "You can't really afford to take a lot of chances in this business. Leave a lot to luck and you wind up in a grave."

Mildred blinked in surprise, her small eyes and large nose making her look a little owlish. "That's just an expression, right?"

"If 'being dead' is just an expression," Gunn answered.

"He's right," Fred put in. "This is a dangerous business, Ms. Finster. People get hurt, or, you know, worse things. It's not as neat and tidy as it looks on TV or in books. This is Los Angeles, not some English country house with a dotty superintendent and a gentleman poisoner."

"Well," Mildred said, sounding embarrassed or hurt by Fred's remarks. "I surely didn't think it was that sort of thing. I saw the poor truck driver's body, remember? Which you didn't."

Gunn picked up the argument again. "That's why I don't understand why you're still nosin' around. You know what can happen."

"I know that without me you people wouldn't even have his name," Mildred countered. "Much less the connection with this mission. Right?"

"That's true, I guess," Fred admitted.

"So it looks as if you're the ones who need me."

Gunn shook his head, trying to look severe. "I'm sure we can take it from here, ma'am. We appreciate what you've done. But I think you should go home and stay there. Whoever did that to the truck driver is still out there, and if he thinks he's gonna go down for that he'll do the same thing to any one of us that gets near him. Including you."

He thought he saw Mildred shiver as she considered that idea. But a cloud had passed in front of the sun as he said it—the first cloud he'd seen in the sky all day—and maybe it was just that.

"I agree with Charles, Ms. Finster," Fred added. "We're used to dealing with these sorts of . . . things. Bad guys, and so on. It's not that you're not helpful—I'm sure you're a wonderful detective. But I'd hate to see you get hurt, and, honestly, we can't take responsibility for keeping you safe."

"Well, I haven't asked you to, have I?" Mildred fired back.

"No, ma'am," Gunn answered quickly. "You haven't. But me and Fred, see, we have this habit of protecting people who find themselves in trouble. We'd probably try to do it for you too. But what would happen if we had to pick between helping you and catching the bad guy? If we had to let him go, and then he killed someone else, how would you feel then?"

Mildred considered this for a moment, looking

toward her car. When she looked back at Gunn her face was different, her eyes clear, her soft jaw set as firmly as could be. "I haven't asked for protection, Mr. Gunn," she said again. "Nor shall I. I'm sure I'm easily three times as old as the both of you, and I got here by taking care of myself, thank you very much. I intend to continue to do so."

"Yeah, but I don't think you've ever messed around with something quite like you're getting mixed up in here," Gunn insisted, not willing to drop the subject. "Try knitting or canasta. Start a book club. Anything but this."

"I appreciate your concern," Mildred said after a few moments. "I will give what you've said some long, hard thought."

Gunn shrugged. "I guess that's all we can ask."

"Thank you, Ms. Finster," Fred added. "We just don't want anybody getting hurt or anything."

Mildred nodded and smiled. "I can understand that," she said. "Now I guess, if you don't have any objections, I'll drive myself home."

"That sounds like a terrific idea," Fred said. "Let's all do that. In our own separate cars, I mean. Except that Charles and I sort of came here together, I guess, so we'll drive ourselves home together too."

Mildred gave Fred a final, quizzical look—almost as if questioning her sanity, Gunn believed—

and got into her car. With a last wave he and Fred headed back to the truck.

A few moments with a phone book told Angel that there was a state parks office in downtown L.A., so he left Cordy and Lorne at the hotel and worked his way to the building's underground garage, then came up on an elevator into their lobby. A polished wood counter faced the elevators, and uniformed employees, looking like forest rangers without the forest, worked behind it. The shipping order for the truck full of mission items had originated at this office. Angel waited in line for a few minutes as other people approached the counter, inquiring about camping permits, park passports, and various issues that made him wonder, not for the first time or even the thousandth, what it must be like to be a normal human being in this century.

Finally his turn came. He was summoned to the counter by an attractive woman with auburn hair pulled back in a ponytail, her bright green eyes sparkling as if she'd just remembered a joke. "How can I help you?" she asked him.

He put his hands on the counter's edge and leaned in, speaking softly. "A truck was stolen yesterday. Driver killed. I'm looking into it. It was carrying cargo destined for the Mission San Alejandro, originating at a parks warehouse up north." He noticed that the woman's smile had faded and that another employee, a man with dark, thinning hair and thick glasses, had stopped sorting folders into a filing cabinet for a moment. "I'm just wondering if you can tell me anything more about it. Any speculation as to who might have wanted to stop the shipment from reaching its destination, or anything unusual about the circumstances of the shipment."

The woman worked her mouth for a moment but no sound came out. "I . . . I'm sorry," she finally said. "I don't even know what to say to that. I can't talk about that."

"Is there a supervisor?" Angel pressed. "Someone who can talk to me?"

"What's he asking about?" the male employee wanted to know. His voice was reedy and shrill.

The woman shot him a glance full of daggers. *These two aren't the closest of friends*, Angel speculated. "That truck."

"You can't talk about that," the man said.

"That's what I just told him, Donald," the woman replied icily. She turned back to Angel with a subtle shrug. "Like I said."

Angel tried again. "What about a supervisor?"

She bent over and came back up with a business card, and slid it across the shiny surface of the countertop to him. "This is our public affairs officer," she said. "All inquiries are to be directed to her. She's not in right now—as you can imagine, this has turned into a pretty hectic week. And she's kind of a dragon lady, at any rate. Maybe she'll talk to you, and maybe not."

Angel pocketed the card, but didn't exactly feel waves of optimism rolling off this woman. "Thanks," he said.

For nothing.

As soon as the pale guy was back in the elevator, Donald Raglin announced that he was taking his fifteen-minute break. He went out the building's front door and then down to the corner of the block, where he was unlikely to be seen or heard by any of his fellow employees. Leaning against a building's wall, he fished a cell phone from his pocket and punched one of his saved numbers. A moment later, the familiar voice answered. "Yes?"

"It's me," Donald began. "You said to let you know if anyone came in asking about that truck. I mean, you know, anyone who's not cops or the press or anything."

There was a long silence at the other end of the line. Donald wondered if he'd been disconnected. "Hello? Are you there?"

"Yes."

"Okay. So, you know, people have been asking about the truck all day, but it's been reporters, a few detectives, you know. It hasn't really hit the news yet, so the crazies haven't come out." He paused again, and again there was no response from the person on the other end. "But this guy—I figured you'd want to hear about him."

"Why is that?"

Finally something other than "yes." Donald felt like he'd been given a gift. "Because this guy didn't talk like a nutjob, you know. He sounded serious, said he was 'looking into' the truck's disappearance. But also, the biggest thing is, when I looked at him and then looked at the counter—and you've been there, you've seen how polished that counter is, we keep it immaculate. Anyway, this guy didn't have a reflection."

Another pause. Then, if the other time had been a gift, this one was a treasure. Still just three words, but they filled Donald Raglin's heart with gladness.

"You've done well."

CHAPTER SEVEN

Charles idled the truck's engine while they waited for Mildred Finster to get out of the parking lot. He had started the vehicle, and put it into reverse to back out of the space, but Fred had reached out a hand on his knee to stop him. Almost as soon as she did so, she realized what she was doing and pulled it back, since it had been simply out of long habit that she'd done it in the first place. As it was, her hand just grazed his leg, but that was enough to make her feel strange and just the slightest bit hypocritical. "Give her a minute," Fred suggested. "Let her get out of the lot first. That's the only way we'll know she's really leaving, and not following us anymore."

Charles had nodded his head in agreement and sat tight while Mildred climbed into her car, adjusted the mirror, fastened her seatbelt, adjusted the mirror again, cranked her head around to see if there was anyone behind her, put the car into gear and started backing up, adjusted the mirror still more, and then lurched out of the parking spot as if it had suddenly become a war zone.

He sat, a smug half-smile on his handsome face, until Mildred was out of the lot and headed back toward the freeway that would take her home. Then he turned to Fred. "She knows where we work."

"She knows . . . ohhh . . ."

"So she doesn't have to follow us. She can just pick us up there any time she wants."

"I understand, Charles," Fred said. She felt defensive, as though he was accusing her of stupidity. *I'm a lot of things,* she thought, *but stupid isn't one of them.* "I thought I had a good idea, but I was wrong. I admit it."

"I'm not trying to make you feel bad, Fred," Charles assured her. She wasn't buying it, though. "Really, that's not what I meant. Just thought it was funny, us sittin' here watchin' her go like it really accomplishes anything."

Fred inclined her face away from him, looking toward her own shoe. She felt flushed, embarrassed. "Yes, it's very funny. Ha ha. Can't you see me laughing here?"

He reached for her shoulder, but she wiggled from his grasp. "Fred, I wasn't trying to . . . oh, never mind." He pulled his hand back, put it on the steering wheel.

ANGEL

Don't give up so easily, Charles. Fred was surprised to hear herself thinking it. But it was true. She couldn't bring herself to forgive him for what he had done—not yet, at least. And her anger showed itself in unexpected ways. But that didn't mean she didn't want him to keep trying. She had put up defenses against him, after what he had done.

But she still wanted him to break through those defenses. Maybe. At the least, she couldn't help wanting him to try.

Donald Raglin showed up where the voice on the phone had told him to. He didn't know either of the men he'd spoken to well enough to tell who was who on the phone, though in person he was pretty sure he knew Mr. Dodds from Mr. Atkins. He parked his car on Figueroa, as the voice had instructed, and then walked around the block, past a few small retail businesses and a travel agency with sun-bleached posters of exotic locales, to an alley that ran behind the buildings.

Back here the noise from the street was muffled, as if he had somehow passed through a veil that had taken him far away from civilization. These buildings were old, dusty brick painted many times over, with remnants of advertising posters clinging to them like bad memories that can't be shaken.

Donald was very familiar with bad memories. They were just about all he had. His mother, he firmly believed, had hated him from the day he'd been born. She had never wanted kids, and she'd made that crystal clear. His father might have been more accommodating, but he bowed to her will in most cases, and finally, when she got to be too monstrous even for him, he had run away and left young Donald alone with her.

Intimidated by his own mother, afraid to have any close friends, Donald had grown up in a cold, unwelcoming world. He had felt like a social misfit, a pariah, and then had played that part through school and young adulthood. After high school he had drifted for a while, without any real direction or purpose, and had finally landed a civil service job. He hadn't expected anything out of a job except a regular paycheck and maybe some benefits, and that's what he got out of this one. His personality still put people off, so he didn't form friendships with his coworkers. Instead, after work he went home, ate a quiet dinner by himself, maybe watched some TV, and went to bed.

On weekends and vacations he went to the high desert outside of the city and shot handguns he bought at pawnshops in downtown L.A. Sometimes his targets were cacti or road signs, sometimes jackrabbits, birds, lizards. Anything he could spot. Anything he could destroy, and in so doing claim a tiny bit of power for himself that he couldn't find in the rest of his life.

ANGEL

It was on one of these trips that he'd met Mr. Atkins and Mr. Dodds. After the day's shooting, tired and grimy but more at peace than he ever was at the State Parks Department during the week, he had retired to a diner in one of the tiny towns that fringed the wide open spaces. He'd ordered a couple of beers and a burger from a waitress who had acted as if he were overwhelmingly, unreasonably demanding. After he'd been sitting for a while, staring at a two-year-old calendar from an auto parts store that hung on the wall, he saw two men walk into the diner, looking as out of place as nuns in a strip club. They sat down at the table next to his.

They were both in their late forties or early fifties, he guessed. One had dark hair combed back off his slender face, with silver frosting at the temples and in the ferocious eyebrows that dominated his ruddy face. The other had an enormous blunt head topped by a crewcut. Both wore navy blue sport coats, open-necked white shirts, and khaki pants, and their leather dress shoes were caked with dirt. The rest of the joint's clientele consisted of dried-out, stringy desert rats and hard-worn laborers, so these two really stood out.

All the more so when the first one, the one with the eyebrows that looked like small, sentient creatures, opened his mouth and spoke to Donald. "I say," he began, and his English accent was immediately noticeable. "We saw you shooting out there today. I said to Mr. Dodds, here, 'Jolly good shooting, eh, Mr. Dodds?'"

Mr. Dodds, whose face was nearly as pale as it was huge, leaned over as if sharing a vital state secret. "And I said, 'That it is, Mr. Atkins. That it is. Man can 'andle a weapon and that's for sure.'"

"So you . . . you guys saw me?" Donald was anxious. He'd been on federal land, breaking federal laws by shooting at non-game animals, with no hunting license, on land where no firearms were supposed to be discharged. If he had been caught, losing his job was a given, and jail time was a distinct possibility.

"Didn't we just say so?" the one called Mr. Atkins asked, lips curling into a bemused grin.

"I believe we did," agreed Mr. Dodds. He rose from his own chair and pulled an empty one away from their table. "Won't you join us, Mr. Raglin?"

Donald Raglin was astonished—and terrified—that these men knew his name. But they were pleasant, and insistent, so he did join them. They bought his dinner, they bought him some drinks, and they treated him like—well, like he thought friends, old *close* friends, might treat someone.

It was an evening that he could barely believe.

They left the little diner after a while and found a saloon, and, taking a table there, they bought more drinks. They talked late into the night. They joked, they laughed. Mr. Dodds and Mr. Atkins told stories on each other. They acted like stuffy British gentlemen, but that, Donald saw, was just the facade they put on. They were as regular as anyone else he'd ever met. And they accepted him completely.

It grew late, and ordinarily Donald would have been back on the road, driving home to Los Angeles. But Mr. Dodds and Mr. Atkins wouldn't hear of that. They found a nearby motel and rented the two best rooms—"best," in this case, being a very relative term, defined perhaps by having no creatures larger than a few spiders living inside— and gave the better of those to Donald.

By the time he climbed into the comfortable bed, head spinning from the alcohol and conversation and the unexpected delight of friendship, Donald was convinced that the two men wanted something from him. He just wasn't sure what it might be.

That mystery was solved the next morning, over a breakfast of steak and eggs and fried potatoes, accompanied by some nips from a silver flask Mr. Dodds kept in his jacket pocket. They did, in fact, want something from him, and they were up front about telling him so. But what they wanted wouldn't cost him anything, wouldn't create any difficulties for him. They just needed some eyes and ears in the state parks office, they explained. There were things going on—they couldn't say what, but hinted at conspiracies and dangerous outsiders and their own very classified official roles, and Donald began to suspect that maybe these two were British intelligence officers, some kind of James Bond types. Probably working, as Bond often did, in concert with the CIA, he decided. He didn't know if they were tracking terrorists or spies or what.

It didn't really matter, though. He already felt indebted to these men—indebted and loyal. He would do whatever they asked him.

Which was how he came to find himself blinking in the bright sunlight of a downtown alley that smelled like trash, in a neighborhood he'd never have ventured into otherwise, waiting to give the full report about the man with no reflection. He was a little nervous about being here, so when he saw Mr. Dodds and Mr. Atkins approaching from the far end of the alley a wave of relief washed over him. His friends had come after all.

"Donald," Mr. Dodds said as they came near him. He offered his hand, and Donald shook it gratefully. "Mr. Dodds," he said. He had never learned their first names—they never used them, even with each other. "It's good to see you."

"And you," Mr. Dodds replied, his usual smile plastered on his face.

Mr. Atkins caught up, and another round of handshakes ensued. Then Mr. Atkins regarded him with a grim expression. "I understand you've had a rather curious visitor?"

"That's one way to put it," Donald answered.

"Tell us about him," Mr. Dodds urged. He sounded anxious.

Donald glanced about the alley, feeling somewhat exposed here. "Should we go someplace we can sit down?" he inquired.

"No, no, this is fine," Mr. Atkins answered quickly. "What did this fellow look like, Donald?"

Donald summoned up the man's face in his mind's eye. "Kind of brown, spiky hair," he described. "Um . . . I guess he was a handsome guy, you know. Tall and broad-shouldered. He wore black."

Mr. Dodds and Mr. Atkins both looked at him expectantly. Donald was put in mind of two vultures waiting for a dying creature to stop moving. After a long moment Mr. Dodds pressed him. "Is that all?"

Donald tried to remember any more details. Most had flown out of his mind when he realized that he wasn't experiencing some kind of optical illusion, that the guy really left no reflection in the countertop. Angela's reflection had been clear as day. But the guy was standing right across from her, his hands gripping the counter's edge. And for him, nothing.

His hands.

"He was pale," Donald recalled. "Like he doesn't get out much. Or like he's been sick, maybe."

"Did he appear to be ill?" Mr. Dodds queried. Both men's voices had an edge to them that Donald wasn't used to, as if this man's appearance had really shaken them up. Or had irrevocably changed things, in some unpleasant but undeniable way.

"No, not really," Donald answered. "He looked pretty buff, you know. But I remember his skin—I mean, I'm pale, and you guys are too, compared to most people in this city. But this guy was even more so, to the point that I really noticed. It was his hands; I noticed his hands were pale, and then I noticed that he didn't have a reflection."

Mr. Dodds and Mr. Atkins looked at each other. Donald hadn't experienced this sort of thing much in his life, but he thought their look was one of shared understanding. "Angel?" Mr. Dodds asked. His voice remained calm but that edge was still there.

"Might well be," Mr. Atkins responded. "Almost certainly, in fact."

"Not surprising."

"Not at all."

"I mean, it is his town, isn't it?" Mr. Dodds went on. "We knew there was a decided possibility that he'd become involved."

"Of course," Mr. Atkins agreed. "Perhaps not quite so soon, though."

"Yes, well, we'll just have to cope with his interference as best we can," Mr. Dodds suggested.

"Of course," Mr. Atkins said again.

"And of course, now he's seen Donald here."

"Right," Mr. Dodds said.

"Compromised him."

"Indeed," Mr. Dodds agreed, with a sidelong glance at Donald.

Donald didn't like what he thought he was hearing. The two men were speaking quickly and without particular inflection, almost as if in code. He wasn't quite following what they were saying, though he tried—the speed of their dialogue and the thickness of their accents and his own anxiety all collaborated to put him about a phrase behind the others. And the surge of blood rushing in his ears made it hard to hear at any rate.

"There's not . . . there's no problem here, is there?" he found himself asking. He truly hoped there was not.

Now Mr. Dodds and Mr. Atkins turned to him, both smiling good-naturedly, and he thought they were about to suggest that they all go have some drinks together, tell a few stories, have some laughs.

Except they didn't. Instead, still smiling, his new friends—his *best* friends—drew handguns out of hidden holsters underneath their navy blue sport coats. They pointed those weapons at Donald.

"No problem at all," Mr. Dodds said, just before he squeezed the trigger.

And in a weird moment of clarity, almost as if everything were moving in slow motion, when Donald had just seen the first flashes at the barrels of both guns but before the sound of gunfire—he never did hear the sound—Donald thought, with deep disappointment, *These guys are just like everyone else after all.*

"Gonna be here all day?"

Startled, Cordelia let out a yelp and mashed both hands down on the keyboard, causing the computer to accompany her with its own chorus of beeps and error sounds. "Geez, Connor," she complained when she was able to get her voice back, "do you have to be so much like your dad?"

From the frown on his expressive face it was clear *that* had been completely the wrong thing to say. "I'm not," he groused. "I'm not like him at all."

Except, of course, in your unnatural strength and speed and agility, Cordelia thought, though she knew better than to say it out loud. *Not to mention a stubborn streak as wide as the Los Angeles basin.*

"What are you doing here?" Cordelia asked, more to change the subject than anything else. Since Angel had thrown Connor out of the hotel, Connor hadn't been around much. To be fair, if any kid of hers had sent her to the bottom of the sea in a cage, she'd be a little ticked as well.

"I saw that he was gone," Connor answered. He didn't have to spell out who the "he" was. "And like I said, I wondered when you were coming home."

This part was fairly new, and Cordy wasn't sure how she felt about it. She had known for a while that Connor was interested in her. But he was way too young for her, and also—and more importantly—he was Angel's son, the impossible result of the union of Angel and Darla, two vampires who should not have been able to reproduce at all. But now that she'd started sleeping at his place, trying to put some distance between herself and Angel until those feelings were all sorted out, he'd begun to behave like a lovesick adolescent—possessive, suspicious, and controlling. *Again, not so unlike his dad,* she thought.

"Well, there's a lot to do here," she explained. Her heart was starting to return to its normal rate. "There's something bad going on, but we just don't know what it is yet. So we're in research mode, trying to find out what we can before things start to blow up in our faces."

"All of this research is stupid," Connor said impatiently. "Why not just go kill it?"

"Because we don't know where it is," Cordelia pointed out. "We don't know what it is, and we don't know who it is. What do you think we should kill?"

"I don't know," Connor said. He paced a few yards away from Cordy's chair, hands stuffed in the pockets of his baggy pants. "Didn't you have one of your visions?"

"Yes, and it showed me an old man," Cordelia observed. "But that's not enough to go on. There are a lot of old men around."

"There's gotta be a way to find out," Connor insisted. "Someone knows. Just pound on the right people until they tell."

You are a lot like your dad, Cordelia thought. But she wouldn't make the mistake of pointing it out again. Instead she simply said, "We're working on it, Connor. Trust me."

"Oh, I do trust you, Cordy. You're probably the only one out of this bunch that I do trust."

"That's a mistake," Cordelia told him.

He spun toward her. "What, trusting you?"

"Not trusting the others. Angel is the most trustworthy man I've ever known. All of them—Fred, Gunn, Lorne—they've risked their lives for me so many times I can't even tell you. You could trust any of them."

Connor shook his head so vigorously that his long brown hair whipped back and forth. "You can trust them, maybe," he said. "Not me. I don't trust easy."

"So I've noticed."

Cordy thought Connor was about to say something else—most likely something that would cement her view of him as unreasonably suspicious of everyone but her, and therefore clinging even more tightly to her than he otherwise might—when the hotel's front door opened. As if the action had triggered some kind of spontaneous physical reaction, Connor vanished from Cordelia's sight.

CHAPTER EIGHT

"Did you say something, Cordy?"

"Who, me?" Cordelia asked, in her "innocent" voice. Which meant, of course, that she was hiding something. Angel sniffed the air as he crossed the lobby. *Connor.* If the boy hadn't grown up so fast, maybe he could've taught him a little more about hygiene. *Kid could use a shower, and maybe a stick of deodorant.*

"Never mind," Angel said, not wanting to press the issue with her. Bad enough that she was staying at his place—he didn't want to put her in a position where she might choose to lie for him too. "You finding out anything?"

Cordelia rose from the computer chair and stretched her arms up over her head, working out kinks. It looked like she'd been at it for a long time—probably hadn't left the computer since before his pointless trip downtown to the state parks office. "I think so," she replied midstretch. Then she brought her arms down, laced her fingers together, and stretched them. "Maybe, anyway."

"What?"

"It's kind of weird," she said hesitantly. "And I'm not sure how it all ties together, if it does. But I was tracing the various mission artifacts that were on the truck, you know? Trying to find out where they had gone, why they were sent away, see if anything had an especially woo-woo, creepy, possessed-by-supernatural-badness kind of history. And I was coming up pretty blank. Sometimes an eighteenth century candle mold is just a candle mold."

"Why do I sense a 'but' in here somewhere?" Angel wondered.

"Because it's coming. *But* you need to be a little more patient sometimes. It's not like, 'Oh, get to the point before I die,' Mr. Immortal."

Angel sighed and parked himself on one of the lobby's banquettes. "Take your time."

"As I was saying, I was looking up the items themselves. But eventually I realized that there was another angle to approach it from—the people who worked at the mission during the time this stuff was sent away. So I started looking into them, and that's when I found something that might be significant." She shrugged. "Or it might not be. But at least it's weird, and since I started working with the Scoobies, and then with you, I've learned that the weirder something is the more likely it is to be important."

"So what was it?" Angel asked, almost afraid to display impatience again.

"One of the rangers, named . . ." She stopped midsentence, turned around, and rushed back to the desk. "I made notes," she explained. She picked a couple of papers up from the desk and returned to the lobby. "Gene Kinross," she said. "He was overseeing the labor crew that was packing and shipping this stuff out, back in 1973 when the mission's big reconstruction project began. According to what I found, he was the one who went through the mission, room by room, and tagged what should stay and what should go, and then he worked with the crew to get everything sent away. All pretty straightforward so far, right?"

Angel nodded, and Cordy continued. "But shortly after the last shipment left the premises, good old Ranger Kinross suffered some kind of attack."

"What kind of attack?"

"I said 'some kind,'" Cordy retorted. "Weren't you listening? If I knew what kind I would have said so, wouldn't I? He went home that night and just collapsed. His wife rushed him to the hospital, but the doctors couldn't figure out what was wrong with him. He was in . . . a coma. I almost said 'some kind' of coma but didn't want to deal with the inevitable 'What kind of coma?' question. The answer is, if the docs didn't know, then I sure don't. Eventually he was released from the hospital, and then the newspapers stopped covering the story, so I don't know what happened to him after that."

Angel steepled his fingers and touched them to his chin. "So you don't know how this ranger's coma relates to the current situation."

"I just told you everything I *know*," Cordelia answered bluntly. "Whether there's a connection . . . that's something I don't *know* know, but I know it. You know? Just because it's too eepy, the timing of the coma, and the way modern medical science—circa 1973, so probably just after bleeding with leeches fell out of favor—couldn't figure out what was wrong."

Angel smiled at her. "I agree with you," he said. "It sounds like something that bears checking out further. Think you can find out if this ranger is still alive, and if so where he is?"

"I," Cordelia said grandly, "have become the queen of Internet research. If I can't find out I'll eat a bug." She made a face at that. "You know, that never sounds convincing when that car dealer says it on TV, either."

Obregon hated the smells that surrounded him. Perfume, hairspray, sweat. The odors of human breath carrying traces of peanut butter, tuna, potatoes, bananas. The tang of blood just under the skin. The dry smell of books, created with technology unfamiliar to him. The ozone stink of electricity running though cables, powering lights and computers and innumerable other machines. The people in the library weren't unlike the people he saw and smelled everywhere he went in this appallingly huge city. At least outside he could escape the human stench, even though he was still surrounded everywhere by people and their concrete, steel, and plastic. The smells they created overwhelmed their own feeble aromas.

But libraries were the place to come for information, and that's what he needed now. The key he had been expecting to find in that truck hadn't been there. Which meant that it was somewhere else. He had to find out where else it might have gone. So he found Los Angeles's biggest library and, after enduring the various odors long enough to learn his way around, secured access to the California History collection. Here there were copies of mission records dating back almost to its founding, some of which brought intense feelings of nostalgia rushing into him. He came across descriptions of items he'd long since forgotten; simple everyday items that hadn't crossed his mind in ages.

They were brought before him in a long line, kept in place by armored soldiers with lances and swords. Flickering light from a dozen torches glanced off the bare skin of their shoulders and chests. They were quiet, subdued, not knowing why they had been brought before him, but probably suspecting they wouldn't like the answer. They all knew what had happened to friends and family members who had been similarly summoned. They had seen the heads piled up against the walls, flesh rotting from them, flies and maggots feasting on eyeballs and tongues. They had dug the trenches where the bodies had been buried, thrown in like kindling onto a fire.

What they didn't understand, what Obregon couldn't convey over the language gulf between them, was the ultimate purpose for which their lives were being sacrificed. They would serve far better in death than they ever had in life, he knew. His own explorations into magickal theory had convinced him that powers unknown could be his by a precise combination of magickal approaches. But to attain that level of power, he needed to sacrifice vast numbers of worthless lower beings to the eldritch nameless ones he would serve.

There was no lack of bodies, though, not here. And with the help of the soldiers he had the political might necessary to see his plans to fruition. Already it was working. He controlled the soldiers, bade them to do his will even where they might once have balked. He even controlled the natives to some extent, enabling his soldiers to herd them to the slaughter like sheep.

Certainly some complained. But he was able to drown out the voices of the dissenters, and to twist their fellows into silencing them even while they stood in line waiting to meet their own fates.

Power, he had decided, was truly a miraculous thing.

After a few minutes he realized that wallowing in the distant past would only delay his search. He turned instead to more recent history. The park's records were detailed, though in some ways the sheer volume of available paperwork just slowed his task. Instead he turned away from the mission records and went to a computer terminal. He spent a few minutes acquainting himself with the technology, mostly by laying his hands on the keyboard and letting the power contained within the computer flow through him. Once he thought he understood it, he used it to access the library's newspaper and periodical records.

"Mission San Alejandro" brought forth too much to be useful, so he narrowed his search. It took a while—the computer didn't think like he did, and while his many years of life had taught him that adaptability was necessary to survive and succeed, he was frustrated by just how stupid these supposedly smart machines could be.

Obregon had dealt with stupidity before, countless

times. In this particular case, though, he couldn't have the computer's head torn off by looping a rope around its neck and tying the other end to the saddle of a skittish mare, nor could he impale the plastic thing on a stake. So he was left only with the option of outsmarting it. And in only a few more minutes he had done so, exposing some tantalizing clues.

He didn't bother with notes—he could keep vast amounts of information inside his head, one of the skills he'd been able to improve during his long period of captivity. When he had what he needed, he left the California collection behind. It was time to move on anyway: The librarian's legs poked out from underneath her desk, just a little, and he didn't think it would be too long before someone saw her there, her neck snapped and a little string of spit and blood running from the corner of her mouth.

Armed with his new information, Obregon hurried from the building and into the bright light of the outdoors.

At the first creaking sound Madelyn Kinross closed her magazine and put it in her lap. She had a hard time reading books, these days; she just couldn't concentrate on any one thing long enough to make it worth even trying. But she liked to read, and magazines could be ordered over the phone and delivered through the mail, or picked up at the town grocery store.

She listened for a moment. Birds sang outside—she glanced toward the window and saw that the day was still bright—and a faint breeze rustled the evergreens that ringed the little clearing in which her home stood, but the house itself was silent. *I imagined it,* she thought. *That's all.* She still had her finger inserted in the magazine, and was about to open it again when there was another sound.

This one was longer, more sustained, a low squeal that seemed to come from the wall directly across from her. She studied the wood-paneled wall, magazine forgotten now but still unconsciously gripped between her tightening fists. A framed painting hung on that wall, a watercolor view of Delicate Arch in Utah. Arches National Park had been Gene's first posting as a ranger, before he'd left the National Park Service to join California's state parks system. Madelyn had seen the painting so many times over so many years that she hardly looked at it these days; it was just part of the background of her life.

But she looked at it now.

It jiggled in place on the wall, its frame clacking lightly against the wood paneling. Then its motions became more abrupt, more violent, as it slammed against the wall. After another moment, it stopped, and Madelyn blew out a sigh of relief.

And then it exploded.

For a brief moment she thought a gunshot had

torn through it, except that was impossible because it would have had to come from inside the wall. Something tore through the painting from behind, then shattered the glass over it and hurtled in her direction. Instinctively she raised the magazine clenched between her fists and blocked the projectile. Across the room the framed picture crashed to the floor. Glass flew everywhere. At the same moment, the nail that had been holding up the painting dropped into her lap.

Her hands went slack and the magazine fluttered to the floor. She picked up the nail. It was a small; it didn't take much to hold up a ten-by-ten-inch watercolor in a narrow aluminum frame. She could barely focus on it, so badly were her hands shaking.

And then there was another squealing sound, and another, and Madelyn buried her head in her arms and bent forward at the waist, trying to shield herself.

Expecting the worst.

Because the sun was high in the sky, Angel let Cordelia drive the GTX with the top up while he huddled in the back, under a thick blanket. The "coma ranger," as Cordy had taken to calling him, lived way out in the San Gabriel Mountains, up above the San Dimas Reservoir. The high country there was thick with pines and hiking trails, but sparsely populated.

A little more than an hour after they had set out, Cordy brought the big car to a shuddering stop in a dirt driveway. "We're here, Angel," she said. "Daniel Boone's place. There's about ten feet of sunlight before you get to the porch, but I can't get in any closer."

Angel shucked off the blanket and carefully surveyed the situation. She was right—a small garden, broken only by a trampled dirt path, stood between the drive and the house. It was a cabin, really, as Cordy had implied with her Daniel Boone crack. Its exterior walls were logs, unpainted and beaten by years of wind and weather. There were also dozens, maybe hundreds, of rocks scattered around. Most were the size of eggs; some were as big as grapefruits, and they were all rounded off as if they'd been in a river. Angel saw fresh chunks taken out of the logs that could have been the result of the stones hitting them. Three rough-hewn steps led to a covered porch, and the door was there, safely shaded. He could make it across the ten feet, under the blanket.

"Let's go," he said. He opened the back door, keeping the blanket wrapped over himself, and ran for the safety of the porch. Cordelia came more slowly, behind him, closing the car doors before she did.

Angel was about to raise a fist to knock on the door when he heard the racket from inside. It sounded almost like a firefight, except the cracking and popping noises weren't as loud as gunfire. Over it he could make out the sound of a woman sobbing, almost in hysterics.

Instead of knocking he tugged on the door handle. Locked. He reared back and kicked at the door, just beneath the handle. It splintered and swung open. He tried to charge inside, but couldn't get past the threshold.

"Cordy," he snapped. "Go in—carefully—and see what's going on. I hear a woman—find her and make her invite me in!" As a vampire, he couldn't enter a residence without an invitation, and there were times when that rule was an enormous handicap.

"On my way." Cordy breezed past him and into the cabin. All Angel could see from here was a kind of entryway, with a staircase leading up and framed doorways going off to the right and left. The woman's keening sound came from the right.

"Through there," Angel instructed. "But be careful."

"Do I *look* suicidal?" Cordy snapped back. She paused at the doorway, peeked through, then went in. Still Angel could hear the unexplained squeals and pops, and the woman's steady lament.

A moment later he heard Cordy's voice. She did her best soothing tones, while at the same time displaying some urgency. "You have to invite my friend in," Cordy insisted. "He can help—really, he can. But he can't come in unless you ask him to. Hey!"

"What is it, Cordy?" Angel called. That had sounded like a cry of distress. "Are you okay?" The worst thing he could imagine was for Cordy to be hurt while he stood around outside, prevented by his own nature from getting in and helping her.

"I'm—ow! I'm fine, Angel," Cordy answered. "Please, ma'am, invite him in. Quick!"

"C-come in," Angel heard. That was enough for him. He dashed inside, through the right-hand door, and into a kind of sitting room.

"Welcome to the madhouse," Cordelia quipped.

She wasn't kidding. As Angel watched, nails from the wood paneling ejected themselves and flew across the room as if they'd been fired from a rifle. Screws from inside the walls burst through the paneling and did the same. Floorboards pried themselves up as finishing nails burst through the wood like miniature geysers going off. A woman sat in a chair, rolled up into a quivering, sobbing ball, bleeding from a score of wounds.

"Angel," Cordelia said, frowning with concern. "We have to get her out of here."

Angel didn't answer, just swept the woman up into his arms. The tang of blood was familiar and tempting but he ignored it, as he had learned to do, and carried her from the room. He took her through the entryway and into the room on the other side, a combination kitchen and dining area. Cordelia followed. Whatever had been responsible for the flying nails and screws had been confined to the one room—everything in here looked fine.

He put the woman down in a wooden dining chair. "Are you okay, ma'am?"

She was able, after a few moments, to lower her hands and raise her face to his. Cuts on her temples and cheeks bled, and her brown eyes and full mouth were pinched and lined by years of worry. Almost as if her absence from the room ended the destruction, the noise faded away—all Angel could hear from the living room now was the dwindling sound of metal screws rolling to a stop on the uneven floorboards.

"Th . . . thank you," the woman managed as she struggled to bring her sobs under control. "Who are you people?"

"My name's Angel," he said softly. "That's Cordelia. We're here to help."

"You . . . you already have, it seems." The woman brushed a stray lock of hair—brown, but streaked with silver—away from her face, but it stuck to the blood from a wound at her left cheekbone. Her eyelids lowered and she turned a deep crimson. "This is . . . embarrassing. Having you come in here like this, and seeing me . . ."

"Please don't worry about it," Cordelia assured her. "You can't imagine some of the humiliating positions we've found ourselves in." Maybe thinking better after she'd said it, she added, "I mean, we've seen lots of people at their worst. And then again, maybe I should just stop trying."

"Why don't you find some hot water, and a clean cloth?" Angel suggested.

"Good idea," Cordy replied quickly, with a grateful smile. "You stay here and do the comforting thing and I'll go to the kitchen for some hot water."

She started to leave the room, but then she stopped. "The kitchen is right here, isn't it?"

In fact, it was. This room, like the living room, was small, paneled in knotty pine. Beyond the table where the woman sat was a counter, and on the other side of the counter, kitchen appliances and cabinets and a window that looked out the back and down a steep canyon. The cabin was homey and pleasant, Angel thought, except for the fact that apparently every now and then parts of it would attack its occupants without warning.

"Got it," Cordelia said, answering her own question. "Water. Coming right up."

CHAPTER NINE

"This kind of thing happens, from time to time," Madelyn Kinross explained. After tending to her wounds, which were all minor, Cordy had taken the woman into her own room and helped her change from her torn clothes into a pair of faded jeans and a bulky green sweater. Now they sat around the table, sipping coffee Angel had brewed while he waited for them. Coffee was an art form he had never entirely mastered, his tastes running toward beverages with higher hemoglobin content, but it was drinkable. He'd poured it into thick ceramic mugs and put out milk and sugar, and when Madelyn finally returned she had thanked him profusely.

"Have you thought about, I don't know . . . moving?" Cordy wanted to know. *This,* Angel thought, *from the woman who wouldn't give up her own apartment, even though she had to share it with a ghost.*

"Not really," Madelyn said. "I never had the feeling it was the place." Her eyes ticked toward her left—toward the room in which, Angel knew from having peeked in while the coffee brewed, her comatose husband lay. "It started after Gene . . . after he got sick. It's only very occasionally, and while it is frightening, it's never actually been dangerous before."

"What have you tried to do about it?" Angel asked. "Anything?"

"Well, at first I went to the police," she said. "You can't begin to imagine how useless *that* was. The government was no help either. Then I tried going to this college professor, down in Fullerton, who had written a couple of books about psychic phenomena. He brought his class up here and they tromped around for a while—darn near ruined my tomatoes—but they never did anything useful. That's why I let you in—I figured, whoever you were, you couldn't be any less helpful than everyone who's tried before. Like I said, things only happened now and again, and it was scary but that's all. So I just kind of put it out of my mind, tried to ignore it."

"You said you don't think it's the place," Cordelia prodded her. "Then what is it?"

"It's him, right?" Angel suggested. "Your husband."

Madelyn nodded. Angel couldn't remember ever having seen someone who looked so weary.

"It started after he came home from the hospital. At first I thought it was someone . . . some*thing* . . . trying to hurt him. But it never does. Even this time he wasn't in danger. If I'd realized that it was only in the living room I might have been okay too."

"Unless it followed you," Cordelia added.

"That's true, I suppose."

"So this is the first time it's really been dangerous?" Angel prompted. "Has it escalated in other ways too?"

"Definitely." She wrapped her arms tightly around herself, as if trying to fend off bad memories. Her forehead furrowed, and Angel had the sense that she spent more time frowning than not. "It used to be a long time between incidents. Sometimes as much as a year, other times three months, or six. But suddenly it's gotten much more frequent. A rain of stones last night. First thing this morning a phantom thunderstorm—all the noise and flashes like lightning, but when I looked outside it was as clear as it is now. It was all inside. And then I was trying to relax this afternoon, and this . . ." Her eyes brimmed with tears. "Why? Did I do something bad? Gene never . . . he's a good man. He never did anything to hurt anyone."

"I'm sure you didn't either," Cordy sympathized.

"I'm no saint, I'm afraid," Madelyn admitted,

shaking her head sadly. "I couldn't keep working, and be here for him. But there have been times that I've . . . you know, a woman gets lonely."

"But if it started shortly after he came home . . . how lonely did you have time to get?" Cordy asked.

Madelyn gave her a smile and Angel could see that, before the years of worry and care had taken their toll, she'd been a lovely woman. "You're right," she said thankfully. "It did start before I ever did anything like that. And it was never very often. I couldn't—"

"Never mind that," Angel said, uncomfortable with the direction of the conversation. "If it started just after your husband came home, that's what's important. That must be the triggering event, somehow. Did you ever find out what caused the coma?"

Madelyn shook her head briskly. "NMC, they said. No medical cause. They tried every test they could think of, and then some. Thank goodness for insurance—the medical bills were just insane. MRIs, CAT scans, everything. They couldn't find a thing wrong with him. Even now—a doctor comes to check him out, every three months—he's healthy as a horse. Except he just won't wake up."

Angel had looked in, briefly, on him while Madelyn changed. "He's not on any life support equipment?"

"No, he doesn't need anything like that. Doesn't

even need an IV drip. He doesn't eat anything, obviously. He should be dead. But he maintains the same weight, the same coloration, everything. It's almost like he's a wax figure, except that his heart is beating and he's breathing."

"That's impossible," Cordelia said. "Isn't it?"

"Yes," Madelyn answered simply. "Completely impossible. Which is why medical science wants nothing to do with him. They hate things they can't explain, and Gene is definitely that. For a while they wanted to study him, but he just wouldn't fit into any of the theories they had. Everyone gave up, little by little. Now, except for the one doctor who comes around, he doesn't see anyone. It's been ten—no, twelve—years since the last one quit."

"This must all have been very hard on you," Angel speculated.

"I never thought of myself as very strong," she said with a sigh. "Not the kind of woman who could bear difficult burdens. Even now I'm not sure how good a job I've done. There are days when it's all I can do to look in on him once or twice."

"But you've stuck with him," Cordelia said. She sounded genuinely impressed. "You haven't abandoned him. You haven't given up."

Madelyn glanced about as if someone else might overhear them. "I tried, a couple of times," she admitted, looking crestfallen. "I just couldn't do it."

"Sounds like you're stronger than you give yourself credit for," Angel suggested.

A shrug. "I don't know, maybe I am."

"Angel, there has to be something we can do about this, right?" Cordy urged him.

His turn to shrug. *I have no idea*, he thought. But he didn't want to say that, didn't want to just surrender like so many others had. "We'll figure something out."

"Do you want to see him?" Madelyn asked.

Angel didn't really see the purpose in doing so again. But she didn't know he had already peeked in. And he was becoming convinced that somehow Gene Kinross was the key to everything that had happened—the truck driver's murder, Cordy's vision. It all led back to him. "Sure."

Gene Kinross hadn't moved since Angel had last looked in on him, but that was hardly surprising. He had a youthful face, with sandy hair and a firm jaw. When Angel pulled back an eyelid he saw clear green eyes. Gene looked decades younger than his wife. "He really hasn't aged, has he?"

"Not since that last day he went to work and got . . . got sick. That's what I call it, since I don't know what else to. He got sick, and he stayed sick."

"Angel, he's like . . . like Sleeping Beauty," Cordelia

put in. "Except for the part where she was a girl and he's . . . not."

Angel thought about that for a moment. "I can't remember what spell was used on her."

Cordy arched an eyebrow at him. "It's a fairy tale, silly."

He arched back. "Shows what you know." He let Cordy wonder about that and laid his hand gently against Gene Kinross's cheek. The man's flesh was warm and soft. He smelled clean. He might just have been sleeping, except that the sleep had gone on for three decades now. It was obvious, despite her protestations, that his wife took good care of him.

"And you don't have any idea what happened to him?" Angel asked, though he was already sure of the answer.

"No, not at all. They told me that he was just working—he had just wrapped up a big project, and when he came home he seemed very tired. I was going out with a friend, but I made him some dinner and tucked him into bed. When I got back, he was like this. I called the paramedics, of course, had him rushed to a hospital. And . . . well, you know the rest. He's been just like this ever since."

"We'll see what we can do to help," Angel promised her solemnly. "I don't know if we can. But we'll try."

For the third time since he and Cordy had been there, tears glistened in Madelyn's eyes.

They stayed for another forty minutes or so, but Angel could see that there was nothing he could do to rouse Gene Kinross, and Madelyn had no idea what, if anything, would have made him a target for these magickal attacks. Or just as importantly, who might have had it in for him. Gene Kinross was, according to his loving wife, an all-around nice guy. He worked as a ranger because he loved nature and the outdoors and history. He had volunteered after working hours, coaching Little League baseball because he liked kids and he and Madelyn had been unable to have any. He was, Madelyn implied, kind to animals and all living things. Which was all well and good, but didn't help Angel any.

They were getting ready to leave when Angel heard a car pull up outside. "You expecting company?" he asked.

"I wasn't even expecting *you*," Madelyn replied, somewhat anxiously.

"That's true."

Cordelia went to the window and peeked out through gingham curtains. "Angel," she said, fear rising in her voice like floodwater in a storm. "I think it's him!"

"You think it's who?" Angel queried.

"The guy. From the . . . you know, the thing."

He was guessing she meant the man who'd killed the truck driver, in her vision. But it was a little hard to tell. "I think it's okay to let Madelyn know you have visions, Cor," Angel said. "It's not like she hasn't seen stranger things."

The car came to a stop in the dirt outside, and a door opened, then slammed shut. Footsteps started toward the cabin.

"Stay in here," Angel instructed Madelyn. "I'll see what he wants. Cordy, you stay with her." He went into the entryway to wait for the visitor.

When the man reached the door he didn't bother to knock, just pushed it open. To be fair, Angel had snapped it so that it didn't exactly close very well anyway. He was older-looking than Angel expected, even though Cordelia had described him that way. He wore a nice suit, charcoal gray with pinstripes, with a white silk shirt that set off his silver hair. Angel half expected him to ask politely for directions in a voice like a cartoon butler's.

But instead the man snarled at Angel. "Where is he?"

"Who?" Angel asked him. He moved a half step to his right, subtly blocking the man's entry into the cabin. If the man was indeed the one from Cordy's vision he'd get a whole lot less subtle in a hurry, but he wanted to be sure.

"The ranger, of course." The man snapped like

he was speaking to a slightly deranged child. His small hands were clenched into fists that Angel couldn't quite bring himself to be afraid of. When he spoke, Angel heard a melange of accents, vaguely European, with a slight whistle on the *s* sound. "Kinross. Who do you think?"

"He's not seeing visitors today," Angel said. "You want to leave a message?"

"What I want is for you to get out of my way," the old man insisted. "Before I lose my patience."

"Too late for me," Angel replied, reaching for the man's tailored suit coat. "Guess I lost my patience first. Sometimes my manners just plain suck."

But the man moved faster than Angel would ever have expected, blocking Angel's reach with his left hand and sliding his right beneath the block. The clenched right fist drove into Angel's midsection like a runaway train. Taken by surprise, the vampire doubled over the fist. The old man brought the hand he'd initially used to block Angel back around, catching Angel's jaw and sending him flying.

Angel crashed into the staircase behind him. As he fell he caught a glimpse of Cordelia, watching from the doorway with the ranger's wife behind her. "Keep her out of here!" Angel shouted. If he was going to have the stuffing beaten out of him, which was seeming like a distinct possibility, he didn't want Madelyn watching it.

But he didn't intend to let it get that bad. He forced himself up off the stairs and hurtled toward the man, who was also coming at him. They met in the middle of the little entryway, hands clawing at each other. The force of Angel's momentum drove the man back an inch, but that was all. Angel broke his right hand free of the man's grip and jabbed at his opponent's jaw. The old man's head snapped back, but he didn't go down or even release his hold on Angel's left. Instead he snarled like a vicious beast and kicked at Angel's knee.

Seeing the kick coming, Angel sidestepped it and returned one of his own, a high snap kick that should have crushed the old man's thigh. The man's speed hadn't deserted him, though, and his reflexes were every bit the equal of Angel's. He twisted away from Angel's kick so that it merely glanced off his leg. While Angel was off-balance from the kick, the old man continued his turn, sweeping his arm around like a baseball bat, and driving Angel into the side wall.

That's it, Angel thought, shaking off the effects of the blow. *Now I'm* really *mad*. He charged at the old man and let the change come over him as he did, his fangs extending, forehead thickening, his inner vamp showing itself. He thought it might shake the old guy, cause him to make a mistake, to lower his guard and give Angel an advantage.

But it didn't work that way. The guy took it in with a casual glance and raised his hands to block Angel's charge. Angel moved in close and threw a right-left-left-right combination. Two of the blows landed heavily, and the old man grunted in pain. This was the first indication that he was getting through, and Angel was glad to see it, hopeful that it meant he'd be able to put the guy down without much more effort. Angel dodged a halfhearted punch and landed another, a right jab to the man's ribcage. The guy's step faltered and he looked at Angel with a new light in his eyes. *Fear,* Angel thought, enjoying the realization.

He threw a couple of punches at Angel, hard ones that shook Angel and reminded him that the old man hadn't given up yet. But then the man surprised him once again. He used the momentary reprieve he'd earned by staggering Angel to back out through the open front door.

Angel followed him out, but the man didn't pause on the front porch—he kept going, down the stairs and out into the bright sunshine. Glancing at the heavy blanket he had worn from the car, discarded on the porch after it had served its purpose, Angel knew that he couldn't fight if he had to don it again. And the sunshine would fry him in seconds, long before he could defeat such a powerful opponent. But he couldn't just let this guy get away, and lose whatever chance he might have had to find out how he was connected to Gene Kinross, as well as to the murder of the Crossways Freight driver.

He dove for the man. The moment he burst into the light, he felt it burning him, as if he stood too close to the open door of a blast furnace. When he reached the old man, he tried to land a punch but the incredible pain threw his balance off. The man caught his wrist in two hands and held on, and Angel realized his plan. He hadn't been afraid of Angel, not for a moment. Once he'd realized he was fighting a vampire his intention had changed. He would lure Angel out into the sun and keep him there, letting that bright star do his fighting for him.

Angel could smell his skin beginning to smolder and knew the man's plan would work if he couldn't free himself. Gathering every last reserve of strength he could summon, he moved in close, bringing his booted foot down hard on the old man's instep. The man squealed in pain and doubled over, and Angel head-butted him with his dense forehead. The man clutched at his head in agony, releasing Angel's wrist.

But Angel couldn't stay to press his momentary advantage. He hurled himself backward toward the porch. He tripped on the steps but clambered up and threw himself into the saving shade. His skin smoked in spots, and he writhed in torment. He knew he had made it in time to save himself, but not soon enough to spare him considerable pain.

"Are you okay, Angel?" Cordelia asked him. He hadn't even heard her come outside and was startled to find her bending close to him.

"I will be," he managed. "But he . . ."

"I'll take care of him." Cordy straightened and stepped out into the sun. The old man waited there, a wide smile on his lined face, smoothing his silver hair back over his head.

"Cordy, no!" Angel shouted anxiously. "He's too strong for you!"

"Part demon, remember?" she tossed back.

"That doesn't make you indestructible."

"We'll find out," she said.

"He's right, you know," the man said in a voice that was almost friendly. "You can't possibly beat me."

"You have no idea what I can do," Cordelia countered.

"I could say the same."

"I know you killed that truck driver," Cordelia said. Even from where he sat on the porch, Angel could see the surprise register on the old guy's face. "That's right. I guess you did underestimate me after all."

"Perhaps," the man admitted. "But I won't any longer." Instead of waiting for Cordelia's move, he lunged at her. She blocked his first volley, but he finally landed a solid blow that slammed her back against Angel's car. She clawed her way unsteadily to her feet, blood already starting to flow from her nose.

"Cor," Angel said, knowing even as he did that it was hopeless. She ignored him and charged the man, using moves Angel didn't even realize she knew. She connected a few times, once driving the man to his knees. But he regained his footing and fought back just as hard.

"You've got to help her," Madelyn Kinross pleaded from behind Angel. He saw her standing in the doorway, watching, a look of horror on her face.

Angel wanted to tell her that he couldn't, that even to step back into the sun meant to risk incineration. But in spite of Cordy's unexpected strength, and what seemed like a ruthless streak he had never seen in her before, the old man was getting the upper hand. He had closed his hands around Cordy's throat, and her face was starting to turn eggplant purple. Madelyn was right, like it or not.

Bracing himself against the cabin's wall, Angel rose to his feet. He couldn't let Cordelia die while he huddled in the shade. Throwing himself off the porch, he caught the man a glancing blow as he landed in the dirt of the driveway. He lashed out with his legs, entangling the old guy's ankles and scissoring, knocking the guy off balance. The man released Cordy, who staggered back against the

GTX, hands at her throat, wheezing and trying to catch her breath.

Again Angel couldn't press his attack. Cordelia was safe, and the sun's rays were too much for him. "Cordy!" he shouted desperately. "Let him go!"

She shook her head urgently, but she was finished, out of the fight. She tried to take a couple of steps forward but collapsed, and the head shaking became a nod of agreement. Angel grabbed her arm and dragged her back to the porch. He reached the shade before he burst into flames, which he took to be of some comfort. And Cordy was alive, which was good too.

The bad part was, the old man stood there in the driveway, basking in the sunlight like a contented lizard on a rock. "You tried," the man said, apparently understanding that his advantage only held outside. "At least you can tell yourselves that, after I'm gone." He glanced at Angel's car. "But just in case you should try to follow me . . ." He squatted next to the GTX, hooked the fingers of his right hand into a claw, and tore through the rubber of the left rear tire like it was paper. The car lurched and settled on the shredded rubber and the steel rim.

Then the man returned to his own car, a recent-model, dark, imported sedan, and climbed in. Angel was helpless to stop him. Madelyn Kinross held Cordelia, who was still gasping hoarsely. When the old man had the door wide open, Angel saw a patch of dark liquid on the dash, and at the same time a whiff of it drifted to him. Blood. *Probably belonged to whomever he stole the car from,* Angel realized, and he wondered just how many victims this guy had racked up so far.

Then the man closed the door, started the engine, and drove away with a final, friendly wave. Angel could hardly remember feeling so helpless, so furious. That guy had hurt Cordelia and he'd just had to sit by and let it happen. His vampire strength had given him an edge—in a fair fight, he still believed he could take the old man—but had made him vulnerable to the sun, and the man had used that against him.

"Cordelia, I . . . ," he began, but he let the sentence trail off because he wasn't sure where to go with it.

"Don't worry about it, Angel," she replied, her voice raw. "There was nothing you could do. I know that."

"But I . . ."

"But nothing. Sacrificing yourself to stop him would have been stupid. And it wouldn't have worked. If you'd gone all charbroiled then he'd still have been able to get away. Or he'd have come inside and got Ranger Kinross, which seems to be what he wanted. At least you prevented that."

"Don't talk," Angel said, feeling his own strength starting to return, even in spite of the pain he still felt. "It hurts to listen to you."

"I've heard that since high school," Cordy replied, still hoarse. "Hasn't stopped me yet. Anyway, it looks like I have a tire to change. You do have a spare, right?"

"It's in the trunk," he said. "But I can . . ."

"No, you can't," she argued. "Unless we want to stay here until it gets dark. And Mrs. Kinross might not appreciate that."

"Actually, I wouldn't mind a bit," Madelyn pointed out.

"We'll arrange some kind of guard duty," Angel promised her. "In case that guy comes back. But we do have to get back to town. We need to try to figure out what's going on if we're going to have any hope of stopping it."

"I understand," Madelyn said, somewhat reluctantly.

"Do you have any idea who that man was? Or what he wanted with your husband?"

"I haven't the slightest," she said firmly. Angel didn't doubt the truth of her words. "I've never seen him before in my life."

"Okay," Cordelia interjected. "If you think of anything, let us know. In the meantime, if you could get me a glass of ice water or something, that'd be great. I'll be changing a tire."

CHAPTER TEN

"We didn't exactly draw a blank," Gunn said. "But we—"

Fred cut him off. "Except that we pretty much did," she insisted. "Draw a blank, I mean. If you think of a blank as being a big zero, a goose egg, nothing squared—"

"I think we can all agree on the definition," Gunn interrupted testily.

Angel and Cordelia had returned to the Hyperion, after Cordy had changed the tire and given Angel no end of grief over the shoddy condition of his spare, and found Fred and Gunn just returning from their trip to the Mission San Alejandro. Now they sat around the lobby area, Gunn leaning casually on the counter.

"But the mission," Gunn went on, "was pretty much of a bust. Didn't see anything weird, didn't find anyone who seemed to know anything about the truck, or was willing to talk about it."

"But we did see Ms. Finster!" Fred interjected excitedly.

"The would-be detective lady?" Cordelia asked.

"That's right," Gunn said. "She followed us out there, I think. We sent her home."

"Did she learn anything?" Angel asked them, remembering how she had been able to extract information from the police at the murder scene, even after he'd come up empty.

Gunn and Fred glanced at each other. "I don't know," Gunn admitted.

"She didn't say," Fred added.

"Just because she's old and maybe a little bit . . . loopy . . . ," Angel reminded them, "doesn't mean she doesn't have some good instincts."

"Yeah," Cordelia added. Her voice had almost returned to normal during the drive home, though there was still some bruising around her neck. "Old people can surprise you sometimes. You should have seen the one who kicked Angel's butt today."

Gunn burst into laughter. "An old lady kicked your butt?"

"It was an old man," Angel shot back defensively. "And he didn't exactly . . . oh, forget it."

"Forget forgettin', sweetcheeks," Lorne said as he entered the room. "We want to hear the whole sordid story."

Angel didn't want to go into it, but he knew that it was important—if not the part about him being forced to give up the fight, then at least the fact that the same man who had killed the truck driver had now targeted Gene Kinross. If nothing else, this confirmed Kinross was connected to the murder and the theft of the truckload of mission furnishings, even if they didn't know why yet. So he told the story, with repeated interruptions from Cordelia when she thought he was leaving out some important detail.

"Man, the smell," she said cheerfully at one point, wrinkling her nose. "You thought burning hair smelled bad. You should smell burning Angel."

"I don't think we need to," Gunn said. "Hearing your loving description of it is good enough for me without havin' the pleasure of the full experience."

Fred, though, was filled with concern, and she knelt by Angel's side. "Are you okay, Angel? Are there any long-term effects to something like that?"

"Other than obliteration?" Lorne asked. "There's a reason Angel's on the pale side. Vamps and sunlight don't mix."

Fred nodded and petted Angel's arm. They weren't telling her anything she didn't know, and she'd felt protective of Angel ever since she'd had to care for the AngelBeast he had become in Pylea.

Afraid she might actually start to cry, Angel decided it was time to change the subject.

"We need to protect Gene Kinross," Angel said. "We drove that guy away today, but he'll be back."

"And his wife, too," Cordy put in. "From what she said there's some weird stuff going on up in them thar hills. I think she needs protection from more than just the old guy."

"What do you have in mind?" Lorne asked. "Need me to whip up a protection spell of some kind? I did enough of them at Caritas to get through one, I think."

"Something more than that, probably," Angel said. He knew Lorne meant well, and some of his spells could be effective. But stronger ammunition was called for, just now. Even though he didn't much like the idea himself. "We need to call Wesley."

A moment of shocked silence greeted this suggestion.

Finally Cordelia broke it. "Are you sure?"

"No," Angel said flatly. He didn't talk much about Wes to the others, but in his own heart he still hadn't completely forgiven his former friend for stealing Connor away from him. He'd been robbed of the opportunity to raise his own son, and the boy had been turned against him, and that was something that he would never forget. He knew Wes had meant well, and was only trying to protect both himself and the boy, but knowing that and accepting it to the core of his being were two different things. There had been a chasm between them, and while it was being bridged, little by little, there was still a long way to go. Everyone knew how he felt, so he didn't see the need to belabor the point. "But, yes. He's the one we need for this."

There was little discussion after that. Lorne was the one who actually made the call, though Angel had wanted Fred to. But Cordelia took Angel aside and pointed out that if Fred did it, Wesley might have the wrong expectation of why he was being called in. And Gunn would certainly have a problem, which could lead to even more strained relations between him and Fred. All in all, there was no good way to do it, but Lorne was the least bad way. Angel couldn't argue with the reasoning.

But when Wesley arrived, less than an hour later, Fred was the first one he went to. Sparing barely a glance for Angel, he gripped her arms while Gunn smoldered on the sidelines. "Are you all right?" he asked her, his lips inches from her ear. Angel could barely hear him, and Angel's hearing was preternaturally acute.

"Oh, yes, I'm fine," Fred answered, a little nervously. "We're all fine, more or less. Angel and Cordelia got a little roughed up, I guess, but that's all."

Wes released her and turned to Cordy. "You're all right, though, Cordelia?"

"Like she said. Nothing a few days at a spa won't fix."

"But you don't have a few days to spare," Wesley speculated.

"Or the price of admission," Cordelia agreed.

Angel noted that Wes made a point of not asking how he was. He returned the favor. Wes had been through a lot of changes. He looked more confident than he had before, as if now he had grown into the rogue demon hunter role that had once been as alien to him as the biker's leathers he'd so uncomfortably worn. He had taken to wearing contact lenses. He hadn't shaved in a few days, something that would have distressed the old Wesley so much he'd have been scratching at his jaw until he was able to run a razor over it. His shirt was a dark plum color, untucked, open a couple of buttons down his chest. He moved with sureness and grace, and Angel knew that he'd be a formidable opponent for just about anyone.

I could still take him, he thought, a little smugly. *But not many people could.*

Wesley looked at the others, standing around him in a kind of half-circle. "You called me," he observed. "I came. What is it you want?"

"It's kind of a baby-sitting job," Angel told him. He could see from the look on Wesley's face how the ex-Watcher was going to take that, so he quickly amended it. "Not *that* kind of baby-sitting."

"What, then? And this had better be important. I have concerns of my own, you know."

"I understand that," Angel said. Having to even speak in a civil manner to Wes, rather than attacking him and tearing his head off, was a strain for him. "It is important. And you're the best person for the job." *It hurt to say that.*

"Go on."

Angel explained about Cordelia's vision of the old man and the truck driver, and then about how Cordy had located the comatose ranger. He described the supernatural occurrences at the Kinross cabin, and the same old man's visit while they were there. He left out no details, including the humiliating part about having to sit on the porch while the man simply drove away.

"So this ranger and his wife, they're the ones you want me to 'baby-sit?'"

"That's right," Cordelia answered. Angel thought maybe she had sensed the discomfort he felt talking to Wes, and stepped in to relieve him of some of the burden. "So no real babies involved at all. I think she's probably a little too old to have any now, and her husband is a little too . . . unconscious."

"And you thought of me because . . . ?"

Lorne picked up the thread. "It's paranormal party central up there," he said. "Someone's got to be there who can try to figure out how to put the kibosh on the kookiness, while making sure that Uncle Fester doesn't come back for another helping."

Wesley's hand went to his chin in a familiar gesture that Angel found strangely comforting. "I suppose I could do some on-the-spot research," he muttered. "Try to deduce the source of the psychic attacks, and possibly find out what put the poor fellow into a coma at the same time."

"While keeping one eye open for the elderly man," Fred chimed in.

"Yes, well, I don't imagine he'd be much trouble," Wesley said. "A little sunlight isn't a problem for me."

His words stabbed at Angel like a sword, and he bit his lip to keep from responding in kind. Wesley was here volunteering his help. He couldn't go off on the guy.

When there was no response, Wesley cleared his throat. "Very well," he said. "If someone can give me directions, I'll go for a long drive."

"While you're doing that," Cordelia said, "I'll see what I can learn about this old coot now that we've had a better look at him."

"Someone with this cat's skills," Gunn observed, "must have left an impression on somebody. Got to be someone talkin' about bloody, broad-daylight car thefts and the like. I'll make a run out to the streets, see what the word is." He glanced at Lorne. "Want to tag along?"

"Sure," Lorne agreed. "You have your sources, and I have mine. Between the two of us, if anyone has seen grandpa, we'll find out about it."

Fred hesitated for a moment, then made a suggestion of her own. "I'll get on the phone," she said, "and try to find out if that stolen truck has turned up anywhere. Or the bloody car Angel and Cordelia saw."

A few minutes later all were scattered in their various directions, going about the tasks they'd set for themselves. Angel sat in his own dark office, elbows on his desk, his mouth resting against his folded hands. He was proud of the initiative they'd all taken, pleased that he didn't always have to be the one to suggest what tasks they should take on, and when.

It almost makes up for the fact that I need them in the first place.

He'd been on the planet for a long time, two and a half centuries, give or take. For most of that time he'd been a vampire. People and other vamps had come in and out of his life all along the way—Darla, Drusilla, Spike, Buffy, Cordelia, and more. But even as they did, he had always known that ultimately, when the chips were down, he was responsible for himself. He had come into the world alone. He would leave it the same way. Any relationships in between were strictly temporary. He had learned to fend for himself, to rely on himself, and he'd been comfortable with that. More than comfortable, it was his preferred way of life.

But today—today, if he'd been alone, he'd have been beaten. The guy might not have been fighting fair, using the sun like that, but anyone who expected others to fight fair was a fool who deserved whatever he got. He'd have killed the old man if he'd been able to, and the man surely knew it. So he did what he had to do to survive, just as Angel would have.

Only he'd been smart enough to figure out a way to win. Angel hadn't.

That was a huge difference.

Then, Angel thought, *he hurt Cordy*. His fists clenched, knuckles white, as he thought about the moment when he thought the guy might have killed her—when he dove off the porch in spite of the certain pain and likely death, because Cordy's life was at stake.

That's when relationships get dangerous, he knew. Inside, or in the dark, he would eventually have prevailed over the guy. He was amazingly strong and a talented fighter, but he was old, and he would have been worn down. Using the sun was clever. Using the sun *and* Cordelia was diabolical. Angel had a pretty good idea how strong Cordy was, though she hadn't truly been tested since the whole higher being bit had happened. But he didn't think she could really hold her own against the old man—a man who was nearly Angel's equal—for very long. The man had played her, and dangled her as bait to get Angel back into the sunlight. And it had very nearly worked.

If I didn't need Cordy in my life, I wouldn't have fallen for that, he thought. *If I was alone, self-contained, like I should be, she wouldn't even have been there. Alone, I could take him.*

Having friends and allies made him stronger in many ways. But in other, very crucial ways, it made him weak.

He couldn't afford to be weak.

"I have to admit, Pookie," Mildred Finster was saying, "I was quite surprised to come out of the mission and see those two young people standing beside my car. I would have turned and run back inside, except that they had already seen me."

Pookie tilted his head so that she could scratch the underside of his chin, and kneaded at her lap with his paws. She kept scratching.

"They're both nice young people, you know. But I felt that they really didn't take me very seriously. Certainly I didn't learn much while I was in there, but they didn't even ask me what I had found out. It's like they don't believe I have anything to contribute at all. When in fact they wouldn't even know the mission was connected if it weren't for my investigative work at the truck stop."

Pookie purred and nudged her hand. She had stopped scratching, but at this reminder, she continued.

"I had to laugh, though, when they made me drive out ahead of them. As if I didn't know where their headquarters is. I think the young lady figured that out, but I'm not sure the young man ever did. Mr. Gunn. What a terrible name. So violent sounding."

Pookie let out a low "mrrrawrrr" sound and twitched his ears, twice. She shifted her hand to scratch between them. "Oh, you're right, I suppose. It doesn't matter so much what they think of me now, does it? What matters is whether I can prove to them that I'm good at this detecting business. If I can crack the case, then they'll have to take me on as an apprentice, won't they?"

Pookie sneezed. "Oh, dear," Mildred said. "I hope you aren't catching cold." She set the cat down on the floor. "I could use a warm drink myself," she said. "I'll brew up a pot of tea, and give you some nice lovely cream, how does that sound?"

Pookie meowed and rubbed himself against her ankles, nearly tripping her as she started toward the kitchen. But she recovered and went in, flipping on the lights and turning on the radio before she filled her teapot with water. It was the top of the hour, and the radio news came on almost immediately.

ANGEL

"In local news," the announcer said after his usual litany of terrors from around the world, "the victim of a fatal shooting downtown today has been identified as Donald Raglin, thirty-six, of Alhambra. Mr. Raglin was an employee of the California State Parks Department's downtown office. It is reported that he went out for lunch at his usual time this afternoon but never came back. Police at this time are pursuing several leads . . ."

"They always say that, don't they, Pookie?" Mildred asked. She had read enough mysteries to know that the police never admitted they hadn't the slightest clue about anything. If they claimed to have leads, then the killer was more likely to panic and make some kind of mistake.

While her water boiled she took the cream from the refrigerator, poured a little into the bottom of her teacup, and then poured some more into a saucer. She squatted down and put the saucer on the floor for Pookie, who purred gratefully.

"That's true," Mildred said. "He did say the poor man worked for the State Parks Department. And that's the department that operates the Mission San Alejandro, isn't it?"

Pookie silently lapped at the cream. Mildred went on. "Do you suppose there's a connection? A dead truck driver, taking goods to the mission. Now a dead parks employee. Never trust a coincidence, that's what I always say." She didn't, in fact, always say that, but she had read it a time or two in her books, and she thought it was a good bit of advice.

She shut off the burner under her teakettle. "Never mind the tea, then," she said, carefully pouring the unused cream from her cup back into the carton. "It looks like I'm off to the mission again. Nothing solves a crime like legwork, does it, Pookie? Good old-fashioned legwork."

CHAPTER ELEVEN

Stan Musgrave looked at Lorne, then down at the sidewalk, then blinked a few times, then looked at Lorne again.

"I know the feeling, pal," Lorne assured him. "Sometimes I'm awed by my own beauty too. But try to focus here."

"I just . . . I never seen anyone . . . like you before," Musgrave stammered.

"He's led kind of a sheltered life," Gunn explained. "If you don't count two stretches as a guest of the state."

"You mean prison?" Lorne asked, sounding surprised.

Gunn turned back to Musgrave, who he'd known on and off for half a dozen years. "He's handsome if you like green, but a little naive, know what I'm sayin'?"

"I gotcha, man," Musgrave said. He was looking

a little green himself, Gunn thought. Musgrave was a scrawny guy with limp blond hair, wearing an open cotton shirt over a T-shirt and ragged jeans. He stood almost deathly still, as if he were asleep but happened to be standing on a street corner outside a Chinese take-out joint. The only part of him that ever moved faster than a snail's pace was his mouth. Prison, Gunn knew, could not have been easy for someone like him—a man had to have fast reflexes there to survive, and Musgrave seemed to have no reflexes at all. Since his last stint Musgrave had been trying to keep out of trouble, Gunn knew. But he still lived on the edge of trouble, close to the streets, and he usually seemed to know what was going down. An hour of looking and questioning contacts had pointed them in the direction of Stan Musgrave, and now they had found him.

"What we want to know, brother," Lorne said, apparently trying to steer Musgrave back to the preferred topic of conversation, "is anything *you* know about a particularly violent car theft today. Probably a carjacking, I'd say, since the inside of it was full of blood."

Musgrave blinked, but Gunn knew that wasn't necessarily indicative of anything. Everyone had to move sometime. "Yeah, yeah, yeah," he said. "I gotcha. I heard all about that, man. It was heavy. Heavy."

"Weight aside, do you have any other details?" Lorne pressed.

"I gotcha covered, man," Musgrave said, slowly curling his lips into a lopsided grin. He seemed to have forgotten any anxiety about Lorne being green and horned, by this time. Gunn knew that he'd probably seen stranger sights on L.A.'s avenues. "This dude I know, he seen the whole thing, you know? He's been talkin' about it all day."

"So you didn't see it, but your friend did?" Gunn said, trying to clarify.

"That's right."

"We need to talk to your friend, then," Lorne urged. "The sooner, the better."

"I can tell you what he said, man," Musgrave countered. "He told me all about it. This dude, he like totally twisted this other dude's head, like almost tore it off, you know? Then he just dumps the other dude on the ground and just takes off with his ride, man. Totally sucked to be that dude."

"Sounds like our guy," Gunn said to Lorne. Then he put a hand on Musgrave's shoulder. "I think we still need to talk to your friend, okay? Like my man says, sooner is better."

"But I just told you the story."

"It's a little light on the specifics," Gunn replied, trying to stay polite. "We need to know where, and when, and just what the thief looked like. Anything your friend might remember that will help us find him. It's important, dog."

"I gotcha, Gunn," Musgrave said. He opened his hands, palms up—the most dramatic motion Gunn had seen from him. "Tell you what, you hook me up, I'll hook you up, see what I mean? Gotta make a livin', you know."

Lorne slipped a twenty from his pocket and stuffed it into Musgrave's hand. "There you go," he said. "There'll be another one after we meet your friend. Best we can do."

Musgrave pocketed the bill slowly. "Yeah, yeah, I'll make it happen. Give me some time to find him, say, three hours. In the parking lot in back of the Red Rooster, on Hollywood? You know that place?"

"Sure, that restaurant," Gunn said.

"Keep away from the shellfish there," Lorne warned them. "So I've heard, anyway."

"They only serve breakfast and lunch, so nobody'll be using that lot tonight. It'll be quiet. Meet him there—his name's Camel."

"Camel?" Gunn echoed.

"On account of his hump," Musgrave said, straight-faced. "He's, you know, sensitive about it, though, so don't bring it up."

"Got it. No hump talk, parking lot of the Red Rooster, three hours from now."

"And then you can find me down here for my

second installment," Musgrave reminded them.

"We won't forget you," Lorne guaranteed him. "Ever."

After a certain point Angel couldn't even see the heavy bag anymore. At first he had mentally superimposed the old man's face on it, and that had worked for a while. But as he'd kept at it the face had disappeared, and then the bag itself had disappeared, as had the gym around him, the plain walls, the hardwood floor. There was only the rhythm of his fists slamming into the bag, the dance of his footwork, the pumping of his shoulders as he threw punches, one after another after another.

His prolonged stretch with the heavy bag feeling sufficient, Angel turned to the speed bag. Again it took a few minutes to find the rhythm, but once he did he flowed with it like a man in a trance. When he stopped and saw Cordelia watching him, he had no idea how long she'd been standing in the doorway. Her face was solemn, as if she'd been watching a funeral procession instead of a friend's workout.

"Hi," he said. "Been here long?"

"Long enough," she answered unhelpfully.

"Long enough for what?"

She came farther into the room, closer to him. "To know that I've never seen you pushing yourself so hard in training," she said. "And I've seen you push pretty hard."

"No pain, no gain."

She shook her head. "That's a simplistic answer, Angel," she said dismissively. "And it's also a dodge. It doesn't explain anything."

He shook his head, wiped sweat from his brow. "I don't understand what needs explaining," he argued. "I'm just working out."

"I've come down here three times, Angel," Cordelia told him. "I stood right there and watched you, and you never saw me. You've been at it long enough to exhaust yourself, especially after the kind of day you've already had. This is not a normal workout."

"Maybe," he said, "it's the day I've had that's driving me to work so hard."

"That's what I'm thinking," Cordy agreed. "But I think it goes deeper than that."

"You and Sigmund Freud?"

"Could be. Here's what I think—"

Angel interrupted, anger rising in him that he recognized was undeserved. Undeserved by Cordelia, anyway. Misdirected, at best. "Did I ask what you think?"

"I'm telling you anyway. I think you feel humiliated by being beaten by that guy who looked like an old man. He looked easy, but he took you. No, shut up until I finish. Then he hurt me, and you had to stand on the sidelines and let it happen, and yes, you hated that and that humiliated you even more. So you're not going to let it happen again, and that's why you're down here pushing yourself half to death. Being beaten is bad enough, being beaten in front of me, and then watching me get hurt, is even worse. Am I warm?"

Angel didn't even know how to answer that. She probably was. But he hadn't analyzed his own reactions that carefully he had just done what his instincts told him to do, which was to come out here and to punch bags until his knuckles were raw. "I don't know, maybe."

"Maybe nothing," she said triumphantly. "I'm on the button and you know it."

Angel shrugged. "I'll stick with maybe."

The sorrowful look he'd seen on her face before came back. "Angel, what you have to understand is that it doesn't matter."

Now she'd lost him. He sat down on the wooden floor, leaning his back against the wall, feet spread before him. "What doesn't?"

"Someone beating you. In front of me. Big deal. It happens. No one wins every time. Not even you. And the fact that he looked like an old man? So what? Not every monster is ten feet tall with big teeth and claws. Appearances can be deceiving, you know that. Just because he looked like an old man doesn't mean that's what he is."

"I guess that's true," Angel admitted with some reluctance.

"Of course it is," Cordelia went on. "But more importantly, it's not shameful to lose once in a while. And it's not shameful to let me take a shot at him, even though he beat me, too. We're a team, Angel. You can't do it all yourself, and you shouldn't expect to. The Powers That Be hooked you up with Doyle, remember? Then I came along, then Wes and the others. There's a reason for that. You're not alone, and the fight isn't just your fight."

"But ultimately," he argued, "I'm—"

"Forget ultimately," Cordy cut him off. "I'm talking about the here and now. I'm talking about you trying to take the entire responsibility for every battle we fight onto your own shoulders. That's disrespectful, Angel. Of the rest of us. That says that you consider the rest of us second-class citizens, somehow less than you just because we're not vampires, all broody and dark and everything like you are. Well, sorry. Higher being trumps vamp, you know? Not that I can fight better than you, 'cause obviously not the case. But I can hold my own, and so can the others."

Angel was rocked by the unexpected fury of her argument. He couldn't even counter it, really, because she was right. He had come to rely on his friends, his teammates, but still he felt that the final responsibility was his and his alone. If they fell, he would be the one to carry on the fight. He would be the last man standing when the final battle came. The others were weaker than he was, he had always believed, and even though he couldn't conceive of a braver and truer bunch of friends, still he had always suspected, in his heart of hearts, that they would one day move on, find other interests, or just die, as mortals did, and he would find himself alone again.

"You're right," he admitted after a few moments.

"Don't go thinking you can . . . what did you say?" She blinked in confusion.

"I said you're right. You're absolutely right."

"Of course I am," she agreed, smiling. "I was a higher being, remember? Learned a lot. You've got to just get used to me being right, because it happens often."

"I guess I have thought of myself as sort of last-resort guy."

"But that's what we all are. The whole team, not just you."

"I guess I get that now," Angel said, feeling somewhat chastened by her diatribe. "Or I'm trying to, at least."

She walked to where he sat and offered him a hand. He took it, and she tugged him to his feet. "That's good," she said, still holding his hand. He was in no hurry to pull it back. "Because there are people dying out there, Angel. There's something going on, and this ranger and the old man—or whatever he is—are part of it. I've been trying to find out whatever I can about demons who disguise themselves as nice elderly gentlemen, but you'd be surprised how short a list that is. So I've come up blank. We need to come up with a plan to deal with this, and we need to do it soon. And we need to do it together."

Wesley sat in the Kinross cabin's small living room, thumbing through various books he'd brought up with him. Madelyn had prepared him a snack and now he sat with a cup of tea as night enveloped the mountain, reading by the light of a floor lamp and sipping from the cup. She had warned him that the mountain evenings got cold, and she'd lit a fire in a Franklin stove, but he'd put on a sweater just in case. The thermometer—Gene Kinross, she explained, had been a bit of a weather buff, and so the house had multiple thermometers as well as a barometer, and outside wind and rain gauges—had read sixty-eight degrees, last he'd checked, so the little stove was doing its job.

There were spells meant to bring one out of a coma, he knew. But their success frequently depended on knowing what had started the coma in the first place. He himself had been in a coma once that Angel and the others had been unable to bring him out of, but his had been the result of exposure to especially strong Calynthia powder. Gene Kinross's had started so long ago that if there were such a precipitating agent, any evidence of it had long since been forgotten. Which made the whole process somewhat difficult. Even more difficult was the fact that the wrong kind of counterspell could end a subject's coma by killing him. That was definitely not the desired result here, so Wesley kept looking for just the right approach.

Lost in a passage of the book, he unconsciously tugged the sweater more tightly around himself. A few moments later he set the book down on the coffee table and rubbed his hands together. He kept reading, though, even several minutes after that when he blew on his hands, then held them against the sides of his teacup for warmth. That, finally, was when he realized that something was wrong. Perhaps the fire in the stove had gone out. He'd stoke it, stir the embers a bit. He marked the page in his book and went to the stove.

But when he opened the little door, the fire still crackled, as hot as ever.

Wes glanced at the thermometer, then, across the wall from the stove. Forty-two degrees. A loss of twenty-five degrees in a matter of minutes. He estimated that he'd been reading for twenty minutes, at the most, since Madelyn had brought him the tea and then gone into the kitchen to work on some dinner. So more than a degree a minute, in spite of the stove.

That wasn't natural.

"Mrs. Kinross?"

Before she could answer, a stiff, icy wind blew a couple of his books off the table. They hit the floor with a loud thump, and between that and the sound of the wind, howling now, a serious storm under way, her answer, if any, was lost. He spun to go to the door and close it, but the door was closed. So were the windows. But the wind that pummeled him was as powerful as any he'd ever felt, whipping his hair and clothes, knocking items off the sideboard, sliding his books around.

"Mrs. Kinross!" he shouted, very concerned now. He took a glance through the window, and in the evening light outside, everything appeared still—the branches on the pine trees were peaceful, the dirt on the ground stayed in place. So the windstorm only raged inside.

Wesley struggled to the doorway, through there into the small entry area, and then into the dining room/kitchen combination. With each step the wind blew more fiercely, threatening to push him back. He had to hold on to the doorjamb with both hands to force his way into the dining room. Finally he could see Mrs. Kinross. She stood in the kitchen, her shoulder-length hair flapping around her face, her own clothing fluttering and snapping like flags, her face frozen in abject terror.

"Mrs. Kinross, are you all right?" he screamed. *She doesn't look very well,* he thought. *But then I suppose neither do I.*

Before she could answer, the wind died as suddenly as it had started. A look of relief crossed her face. Wesley thought that relief was a little premature, since the cabin's temperature seemed to have dropped still further during the brief interior storm. When she spoke, he could see steam. "You never really get used to it," she said. "But that one's actually happened before."

"I'm not sure it's over yet," he warned. "The temperature . . ."

"Yes, you're right," she said. "There's probably more to come."

"Forgive me for asking, but how can you live like this?"

"I said you don't get used to it," she explained with a wan smile. "But you can learn to live with just about anything, I'm convinced. Some people get by with much less than I have. I have the mountains, the birds and the squirrels, and the coyotes at night. Money's not a problem, with Gene's insurance. I have a few friends. I have Gene, and though he's not much of a conversationalist he's a great listener. These . . . inconveniences are rare, not the norm. I get by."

"They seem to have become considerably less rare," Wesley suggested. "Isn't this the second one today?"

"Yes," Madelyn admitted. She wrapped her arms around herself and rubbed for warmth. "That's right, they do seem to be picking up."

"How long will this last, do you expect? The bitter cold, I mean."

"Hard to say," she replied. "Maybe ten more minutes, if that. It's uncomfortable, but I've never actually suffered frostbite or hypothermia or anything."

Wesley rubbed his nose, which felt in danger of freezing and breaking off. "First time for everything."

"Like I told your friends, it's very annoying, and usually extremely scary. But there never seems to be any real danger. Today, when that nail came through the picture at me, that was the closest I've been to being hurt, I think."

"You . . ." He gestured toward the bruises and cuts that were visible on her face. "You were hurt, today."

Her hand, almost unconsciously, drifted to her face and touched the wounds. "Yes, I suppose I was. Not badly, though. More . . . I don't know. Marked?"

"Like it's claiming you," Wesley speculated.

"Maybe something like that."

"But why? What?"

"If I knew that, Mr. Wyndam-Pryce, I'd—"

"Mrs. Kinross," Wesley said urgently. He pointed behind her but she just touched her face again, as if he were trying to tell her that she had some food on it. "Madelyn—"

When she didn't move, he dove and tackled her, waist high, driving her to the kitchen floor. She screamed.

But the meat cleaver that he had seen levitating from her wooden knife block sailed harmlessly over them and slammed into the wall instead of into her skull, which is where it had been headed.

Of course, now the other knives were on the move. . . .

CHAPTER TWELVE

She's right.

She's also right about it not being the first time she's been right, and it won't be the last.

One thing about Cordy—she's never been afraid to speak her mind. And in the middle of what could seem like free-associative streams of monologue, there are often nuggets of truth that wouldn't even occur to other people.

Energized by his conversation with her, Angel had showered quickly and headed out into the streets. She *was* right. He didn't have to do it all himself—shouldn't even be laboring under the belief that he did. Even now Gunn and Lorne were out looking for a line on the old man, Cordelia and Fred were trying other angles, and Wes—even Wes, who had stolen his son from him—was doing his part, standing watch over the Kinross place.

She was also right about the fact that this was a

situation that needed to be dealt with sooner rather than later. He didn't know who or what the old guy was, but he was definitely more dangerous than he seemed, and he seemed to be a one-man killing machine. Having him loose in the city would have been bad under any circumstances, but having him loose and apparently tied to something so sinister that it generated her first vision in weeks was worse yet.

So he had gone into L.A.'s evening streets to see if he could turn up anything where Lorne and Gunn couldn't. He knew they had a meeting scheduled with a supposed witness to the old guy's carjacking, and maybe that would pan out. But it was too late to rely on maybes. He wanted some definites. To get them, he'd stir things up. If the old man had any friends, then he'd hear that Angel was looking for a rematch. If he didn't, then surely someone had seen him somewhere. He was a lot of things, but he wasn't invisible.

The hour was still a little early for most of the city's unnatural inhabitants—the bars and nightclubs that catered to that specialized set weren't open yet—but there were a few places he could try. He knew, for instance, of a cosmetic surgeon who treated would-be Hollywood stars by day—real stars could afford better work than this one provided—but by night practiced his craft on patients of a less human sort. When demons wanted their ears tucked or some extra weight liposuctioned away, they went to see Dr. Kyle LaMott in his upstairs office suite below Sunset.

Patients were supposed to buzz in at street level, after which they'd be allowed inside, where they could take an elevator up. But Angel didn't want to announce himself, so he waited until someone was coming out of the building and he grabbed the door before it swung shut. In the elevator he punched the button for the third floor and rode up. LaMott had the whole third floor, so he knew that as soon as the doors opened the action would begin. He was still pumped from the workout, and ready for anything.

What he saw, when the doors slid open, was a very plush waiting room with velvet couches, an assortment of magazines on a table, soft music playing in the background, and a nurse's station/check-in counter across the way. Two demons sat in the waiting area. One had a slate gray face that looked like it had been scraped over the proverbial twenty miles of bad road: Angel saw what looked like raw, open wounds, bubbling boils, and scar tissue that pulsated as if living things crawled under the skin. Her ears were ragged flaps of skin that hung limply at the sides of her head. He caught a whiff of her and she smelled like something that had already died.

The second one glanced quickly at Angel and

then turned away, as if embarrassed to be seen there. He wasn't nearly as bad off as the first one, at least to Angel's original estimation. He looked almost human. But even if one thought he was human, there were still little things—the tightness of the skin, the sharpness of the nose and chin, an odd shape to the eyes—that would cause the viewer to believe he wasn't quite normal. He wore a floppy hat beneath which strings of dark hair hung down, surrounding his cheeks, the bones of which almost showed through nearly translucent skin. A paper surgical mask dangled by its elastic thread below his chin.

Angel walked past both of them to the counter. A nurse—human and huge, with a shaved head, a small goatee, and arms the size of redwood trunks—glared at him. "You don't have an appointment," he said, biting the words off angrily. "And you didn't buzz."

"That's because I'm not here for treatment," Angel said. "But I need to see Kyle."

"Dr. LaMott is with a patient," the nurse explained.

"Kyle's license was suspended two years ago," Angel countered calmly. "It's just that most of his patients don't know or don't care. So calling him 'doctor' seems like a bit of a stretch. Anyway, he'll see me."

"I don't think so," the nurse replied.

"It's an emergency," Angel said. He let his inner vampire show, then reined it back in. "See? Can't control my face."

"Vamp. Big deal. We see ten a week. Fang filing, forehead smoothing—you'd be surprised what a little BOTOX'll do for that. Sometimes Dr. LaMott even does forehead implants. Makes for a scarier look."

"Okay," Angel said, quickly losing patience. "Which room is he in?"

The nurse came up off his stool. He was taller than Angel by a good eight inches, and outweighed him by fifty pounds of gym-sculpted muscle. "I said, he's busy."

"You really don't want a scene," Angel said. "Because I might break something, other than your arms, I mean, and I'm not sure that Kyle's in good enough financial condition to renovate the office after I'm through. So just tell me where he is, or sit down and keep quiet while I look for him."

The nurse examined Angel closely, as if he could determine the extent of his threat through visual inspection. Angel stood, hands loose at his sides, and let him look. Finally the nurse asked, "You got a name?"

"Tell him it's Angel."

"Angel?" the nurse repeated. There was a quake to his voice now.

"That's right."

The nurse inclined his head toward the door that separated the waiting area from the examining rooms and surgical suite. "Go on back," he said. "Room five."

Sometimes a reputation is a handy accessory, Angel thought. He pushed through the door and went back, but before he reached room five Kyle LaMott came out, his hands held up in front of him, clad in bloody rubber gloves. He was human, in his late thirties and handsome, with thick dark hair and a jawline that Angel suspected might have had some work done on it by someone more skilled than himself. He wore a blue operating gown and paper booties over his shoes. The smell of antiseptic was almost overpowering. "Angel," he said, sounding surprised. He nodded toward his hands. "Forgot something."

"Shouldn't a nurse get it, so you don't have to leave an operation like that?" Angel asked him.

"The nurse quit. Last week. Demon put a hand—well, a tentacle—on her where it wasn't appreciated, and she just took off."

"Imagine that," Angel said.

"Yeah. Lars is good on the front desk but no use at all in the OR. Anyway, great to see you and all, but I've got someone in there who needs to be minus a head fin when he wakes up, or I'll have yet another malpractice suit on my hands."

Angel moved to block the door to the supply

closet LaMott was trying to get to. "This'll only take a minute," Angel said. "Then you can get back to your unlicensed operation and I'll be out of your hair."

"You do have a mean streak," LaMott said with a forced grin. "What is it?"

"An old man. Or someone who looks like an old man. Very strong, and a killer. You done any work on anyone recently to make them look like that?"

LaMott chuckled nervously. "Most of my patients want to look young, not old. You know that."

"Most doesn't mean all."

"In this case it does. Some don't care if they look their age, Angel. But I don't know any who want to look older than they are."

"It'd be a good cover," Angel suggested. "Make him look distinguished, like some kind of proper elderly gentleman. People would underestimate him."

"Maybe so," LaMott agreed. "But maybe he's just old, too. Doesn't have to mean weak, necessarily."

"That's true. They usually go hand in hand, but I suppose there are ways around it."

"Look at us," LaMott urged. "You're a vampire with a soul, I'm a human whose patients are mostly demons. Anything's possible."

Angel found that he believed LaMott. "And you haven't heard anything about this guy from your patients? I know they talk to you."

"You might be surprised," LaMott told him. "The ones that talk a lot tend to talk about themselves. Pretty self-centered bunch, my clientele. But if I hear anything, I'll get word to you, okay?"

Angel nodded grimly. "Make sure you do."

LaMott made a boy scout's gesture with his bloody gloved fingers. "Scout's honor," he promised.

Angel moved away from the supply room door and back toward the waiting room. "You were never a scout," he said as he went. "But spread the word around. Tell everyone I want this old guy and I'm not letting up until I get him."

Wesley shoved Madelyn Kinross out of the kitchen area, hoping that the counter separating that from the dining room would be sufficient to protect her from flying cutlery. As he drew his hand back after the final push that sent her skidding across the floor, a carving knife thudded into the floorboards where his hand had been and stuck there, vibrating. He turned so that he could see where the other knives were, but not in time to keep a steak knife from flying into his leg just above the knee. He let out a grunt of pain. *And she said these events were never dangerous*, he thought as he drew the utensil out. *It's not as bad as having your throat slit, but it's certainly no picnic.*

He yanked the knife free and threw it to the floor. Blood flowed from the wound, and he yanked a dishtowel down from the refrigerator door, wrapping it quickly around his thigh as a makeshift tourniquet. The other knives circled in the air, moving fast enough to make whistling noises, as if looking for prime targets.

"Are you okay, Wesley?" Madelyn asked him from behind the counter.

"Fine, thanks," he said. "Flesh wound. Everything all right over there?"

"Yes, so far," she said. "What can I . . ."

"Just stay there!" he commanded. "Don't move."

Which was all well and good, but he still didn't know what he was going to do about the serrated-edged air force overhead. If they all came at once he'd be a pincushion. He glanced about the kitchen looking for something he could use to bring them down on his terms, and then his gaze rested on a cutting board, the kind built into the counter that slides out like a wide, flat drawer.

Will moving draw their attention? he wondered. But if it did, grabbing and tying the towel should have. So he lunged for the cutting board, yanked it from its slot, and then, trying to time it just right, stood on unsteady legs and held the board so its flat surface was in front of his face. One after another, the knives thunked into it. One of them took a slice of his finger, but the whistling stopped, and when he dared to look, all the knives were embedded in the board.

There didn't seem to be any further supernatural activity that he could see. "Mrs. Kinross?"

"Yes?" she asked, her voice weak and fearful.

"We seem to have things under control."

She stood up, using the counter to balance herself. Her face was drawn and pale, but she looked grateful. "That's a relief."

"Except," Wesley said, "do things ever happen in different rooms at the same time?"

Horror twisted her features. "Not before," she said. "But there's never been this kind of danger before either!"

"Come on," Wesley urged. But she was already on the move toward her husband's room, ahead of him.

Really what Wes expected to see there was Gene Kinross, slumbering away as usual in his bed, covers pulled up over his chest, hands calmly at his sides. That was what he'd seen each time he'd looked in on the man before. The room was clean, practically sterile, and there was no-longer-used medical equipment under plastic sheeting in one corner, the bed, a dresser with a lace doily on top and fresh flowers in a vase on that, and the big easy chair in which Madelyn sometimes sat to read to him or visit with him. Except for the sleeping man, it barely looked like an inhabited room at all, and

Wesley couldn't quite imagine it changing much.

So he was surprised when he and Madelyn reached the doorway and peered in.

The dresser had been pushed away from the wall. The doily was in tatters and the vase was on the floor, its yellow flowers crushed as if under a boot heel. The big chair had been upended. The plastic over the medical equipment was torn and stained with what looked like rusty water or old blood. But most disturbing of all was the bed, which had flipped up at its head, where it met the wall, so its foot was almost at the ceiling.

And it was pressed flat against the wall. Wesley could see the bed's underside from the doorway, springs and slats and mattress. But Gene Kinross was nowhere in sight.

Which meant that he was between the bed and the wall, where there was precious little space. He would surely suffocate there, Wes knew, in a matter of minutes.

"Oh my God!" Madelyn screamed. She ran to the bed and yanked at it. But it wouldn't give under her efforts; whatever force held it up was stronger than she. Wesley joined her, guessing as he did that it would prove useless. He was right. All the strength he could bring to bear was no good—if anything, the bed pressed itself even tighter to the wall. He was amazed that there was room for anyone between bed and wall, but Gene's limp hand flopped in the empty space, proving that he was still there.

"We've got to get him out!" Madelyn cried. She tugged at the hand but couldn't budge him.

"Yes," Wesley agreed. Obviously, though, brute force wasn't going to do it. Instead he sat down on the floor in the center of the room, folding his legs beneath him, placing his hands on his knees, palms up, fingers touching lightly. Madelyn looked at him as if he'd gone insane, tears rolling down her cheeks, still clutching the lifeless hand of her trapped husband. He ignored her and began to chant.

The words were Sumerian, incredibly ancient. Madelyn couldn't have had the slightest idea what he was saying. Wesley himself only knew the loosest translation. But that didn't matter—the speaking of them, the appropriate intonation, that was what counted. And the mindset of the one doing the chanting. Wesley let the room fade from view, imagining himself instead in a harsh desert landscape, dunes rising all around, wind kicking up plumes of sand at their crests, the afternoon sun an enormous ball of flame overhead. Smoky odors of incense and thick, black tea tickled his nose. The Sumerian words he chanted began to echo back to him, but in voices that were not his own, voices whose owners understood what they signified.

When he reached the end of the chant he blinked

and the room in the Kinross cabin swam back into focus. The bed had righted itself. Madelyn Kinross was draped across her husband's chest, sobbing loudly.

"Is he . . . ?" Wesley didn't want to finish the question.

Madelyn looked over at him with liquid eyes. "He's fine," she said. "I mean, you know . . . he's the same as ever."

Wes blew out a sigh of relief.

"What did you . . . what was that?"

"Ancient spell to counteract supernatural danger," he explained, knowing she didn't require much detail. "Bit of a catchall, I'm afraid, but I don't know enough yet for anything more specifically tailored. It seems to have worked, at any rate."

"Yes . . . thank you," she said, sniffling. She wiped her eyes with the end of her sleeve.

"Quickly now, while the magick is still fresh, I want to do something else," he said. "You'll be all right if I'm more or less incapacitated for a few minutes?"

"I . . . I think so."

"Good." The only way he could think to describe what had happened here was magick, and he knew there was a way to trace the magick to its source. But it had to be done while there was still a resonance of the magick here in the cabin, which meant there was no time to spend comforting Madelyn Kinross. Her husband was alive, and apparently no worse off than he had been, so that would have to do for her.

Instead of the ancient Middle East, the roots of this spell were from the barren steppes of the frozen north, where Siberian shamans had handed it down from generation to generation. Instead of chanting phrases lost in the mists of time, this spell called for meditation and a strict regimen of controlled breathing designed to induce a near-instantaneous trance. With his legs still folded, Wesley began the breathing: three sharp intakes of breath, then one slow exhalation, hold, three in again. At the same time he worked to empty his mind.

Within moments the room was gone again, and he stood in a field of white. In the distance stood a yurt with a thin trail of smoke suspended over it in a still sky, and beyond that, a single, stunted tree. Snow flurried around him; the flakes, when they brushed against him, were soft as a lover's kiss, soft as whispers, soft as dreams. The snow blotted out everything else; sky and land blended together, white on white, without a spot of color anywhere. He couldn't even see himself, could only sense himself, sense that he trod this bleak, blank landscape.

But as he watched, a thread of gold appeared in the sky, drifting down toward him. That, he knew, was what he sought. That thread would lead him to the source of the magick, and therefore, he believed, to whoever or whatever had targeted the Kinrosses. He waited, seemingly a very long time, as it slowly wafted his way, until finally he knew even without being able to see his hands that he could reach it. He closed a hand he couldn't see on the thread and followed it on equally invisible legs. It seemed that he walked for a very long time, but after a while the world ahead—from which the golden thread emanated—became less white, began to take on some kind of substance. As he grew closer he was once again able to see his own limbs and to feel some sense of solidity in his own being.

Finally he took a step that put him back into the world from which he had come. No longer on a windswept steppe or sitting on the floor, he was on his feet, and still in the cabin's tiny bedroom. He still clutched the thread in his hands, but the other end of it was now within sight. It was insubstantial now, not a real thread at all but just a streak of color in the air before him.

And it came from Gene Kinross.

Angel's cell phone rang and he pawed it from his pocket, flipping it open. "Yeah," he said.

"Angel, it's me," Fred said, sounding excited by something. "It's Fred, I mean."

"Hi, Fred."

"Angel, I think I've got something."

"What is it?" he asked. He hoped she was right. His evening had been a bust. Kyle LaMott had been useless. After that he'd broken up a floating craps game he knew about. In addition to being held at constantly changing locations, like most floating craps games, this game was played on a mystical table so the dice seemed to float off the ground. It was supposed to make cheating impossible, as loaded dice would simply fall through the table onto the floor, but he'd never been convinced. Either way, though, no one had been able to supply any information about the old man. He hoped word would somehow filter back to the guy that Angel was on the case, but there was no guarantee of that.

"That truck? The one that was stolen?" Fred asked, as if he'd forget the truck that had started this whole thing in the first place.

"What about it?" Angel wasn't trying to be brusque, but sometimes Fred took her time getting to the point. He didn't have the patience for it tonight.

"I've found it," she told him.

That was worth waiting for. "Where?"

"A warehouse. The owner had an appointment there, and never came back home, so his wife called the police. When they went to check the place out, they found the owner's body and the truck. In pieces."

"How many pieces?" he asked.

"Apparently a lot. So many that the crime scene technicians aren't even going to try to work the scene tonight. They'll do it tomorrow, when they've got daylight and a bigger crew. They took the body out, according to what I've heard, but the rest of it will be there overnight. Under police guard, of course."

"Of course."

"But still, I thought you would want to know."

"You thought right, Fred. Thanks." He hoped he sounded genuinely grateful enough to make up for being short with her. "What's the address?"

"Do you have something to write with?" she asked.

"Fred." Short again. "The address."

"I'm just trying to be helpful, Angel," she said. When he didn't answer she gave it to him. "Got it?"

"I got it. Thanks again, Fred. That's really good work." *Don't want to go overboard with the praise,* he thought. *Maybe one more, though.* "Good job."

He could practically hear her beaming as she hung up.

CHAPTER THIRTEEN

They called him the Solitary Man, he knew. Guards, under strict orders not to speak with him, sometimes forgot themselves, and he'd been told that he was the last prisoner incarcerated in this particular facility. He had known, of course, when his cell block had been emptied. The last prisoner here had been Ulery, Jimmie Ulery, and when they'd come to take him out Obregon had suggested, mentally, that Jimmie try to make a run for it. He had implanted the idea in poor Jimmie's head, and poor Jimmie had tried to grab a guard's gun and had earned himself six bullets for his trouble.

But at least Jimmie Ulery got out, one way or the other. Obregon didn't have that luxury. He watched his guards age, met the new ones, and did what he could to corrupt them because it was one of the only entertainments he had left. He was allowed to watch a certain amount of TV, to read news magazines that were months or years out of date, and occasionally to listen to classical music or light jazz, which he believed was meant as punishment. But playing with the minds of his guards was far more satisfying. They carried wards against just such an event, of course, and regular protective spells were cast. He hadn't much to do, and plenty of time in which to do it, so he always managed to find a way around those spells.

Even that amusement paled after a while, though. So years passed, and then some more, and he waited and waited.

Biding his time . . .

The Red Rooster looked lost and forlorn on Hollywood Boulevard at night. Most businesses along this stretch were lit up and bustling, but since the Rooster—a longtime Hollywood landmark and power breakfast location—closed up after the lunch trade, and was flanked on both sides by office complexes there were empty for the night, there were only a couple of wan spotlights illuminating its fake adobe walls. The familiar red neon sign with its cartoon rooster was dark, as if the rooster were sleeping, or possibly in mourning.

"What I said about the shellfish?" Lorne said as he and Gunn stood on the sidewalk in front of the building. They'd found a parking space in front easily. "It's just hearsay."

"You ever eat here?" Gunn asked him.

Lorne shook his head. "Some places it's hard to get in to when you're green."

"Know the feeling," Gunn agreed. "Not green, but, you know."

They stood there a moment, Lorne taken by surprise at the realization that even in the modern world Gunn would have experienced prejudice based on the color of his skin. Green, he could kind of understand on a basic level—there just weren't many green-skinned, horned folks walking around the streets of L.A. He was definitely from someplace *other*. But there were plenty of African-American folks around, and Lorne couldn't quite get his mind around the idea that some people would make up their minds about a fellow human based on the color of his skin, the accent of his words, or the place from which his ancestors had come. *It's what's inside that counts*, he thought, *clichéd as that sounds. Each of us is an individual, more than just a collection of hues and backgrounds. We all stand alone inside our skins, but we gain power by standing together.*

"Let's go around back," he said simply, leaving the rest of it unspoken. He was proud to know Gunn, and to fight beside him, but it would just make Gunn self-conscious to say so. "And meet someone named Camel."

Gunn flashed a handsome smile. "Just don't mention the hump."

"Wouldn't dream of it, darlin'."

The restaurant was a stand-alone building, set back from the street by a gravel-strewn cactus bed. Against the white mock-adobe walls, below thick leaded-glass windows, juniper bushes hugged the building. A narrow walkway led around the restaurant's left side, and they went that way, past a free-standing air-conditioning unit that hummed softly in the quiet night. On Hollywood Boulevard, passing cars rumbled by, with occasional snatches of loud hip-hop or heavy metal snapping at them like snarls from a penned dog. But as they made their way to the back of the building, where an unevenly-paved alley ran between street-front businesses and a block of apartments, Lorne had the sense that they were stepping into a different place altogether. The street sounds faded as they left Hollywood behind, replaced by the low drone of someone's TV coming from an open apartment window. He could make out the manic roar of a recorded laugh track and realized that he was surrounded by Hollywood—the real thing behind him, its singular product ahead.

Shaking off a vague sense of unreality, he looked through the shadows of the restaurant's chained-off parking area for Camel. After a few seconds

Gunn grabbed his arm, startling him. "There," Gunn whispered, pointing.

At first Lorne couldn't see what he was pointing at. The restaurant's garbage Dumpster stood there in a corner, reeking of kitchen grease and spoiling food. But when he took a couple of steps forward and his eyes adjusted better to the dim light, he saw what Gunn had spotted first. A pair of legs stuck out from the slender strait between the Dumpster and the restaurant's back wall. One of them was fully extended, toe pointed in an almost balletic pose, but the other was curled up, bent at the knee and resting partly on the straight one. It could have been someone sleeping, Lorne knew. But he didn't think so, and suddenly he didn't think that all the stink there came from the Dumpsters.

I hate this part, he thought. *The death, the waste . . .*

"Camel?" Gunn said questioningly. "You okay, man?"

There was, of course, no answer. "This ain't good," Gunn breathed.

"Definitely not." They approached the body cautiously, not knowing where the killer was or if Camel had, in fact, been murdered—or even if this was Camel. So many questions, and the only answer the desperate finality of a dead body.

It was Camel. That was easy to tell when they

reached him. He was, like Stan Musgrave, a slender young man, but with a misshapen shoulder that ballooned his sweatshirt and explained the nickname. The sweatshirt's front was further marred by four neat bullet holes rimmed in blood, its back ripped by exit wounds and black, in the dim light, from soaking in a pool of the stuff. Crouching over the body, holding Camel's arm to inspect him, Gunn looked up at Lorne. Their eyes met but no words passed between them, and none were needed. Their one potential lead to the old man had become a victim himself, and the guy's body count continued to rise.

Gunn released Camel and worked his way out of the narrow slot. "Now what?" he asked. "See if he told Musgrave anything more'n he already told us?"

"If Musgrave is still among the breathing," Lorne replied, the idea that he might not be hitting him with horrible clarity. "Otherwise it looks like we're at, if you'll pardon the inappropriate but nonetheless apt pun, a dead end."

The sound of footsteps in the alley surprised Lorne and he felt his heart leap. But he calmed a bit when he saw two men, instead of a single elderly man, walking casually toward them. They passed through a patch of stray light from the apartment building, and he could see that they were middle-aged, one slim and tall, the other massive, built like an industrial freezer with a head like an anvil. Both wore dark blazers over light shirts, with tan pants. Lorne got a sense of British public school uniform from them.

"Have you found something?" the thin one asked. His accent confirmed the British part, anyway, if not the public school part.

Gunn took the question. "Yeah, you got a cell phone? Someone needs to call 911. It's too late to help him but it's gotta be reported."

"Momentarily," the walking icebox said. Also British. "We'd like to ask you gentlemen a few questions first."

"You guys cops?" Gunn demanded.

The big one laughed. "Hardly."

"Then we got nothing to say to you. You callin' 911 or am I?"

The slender one disagreed. "I think we have much to discuss. We know that this young man was meeting someone here. Now we've had a look at you, we're quite certain that you're the ones he was here to see."

Lorne could sense Gunn's muscles coiling beside him, ready to fight. Running sounded good too, but he made an effort to avoid either scenario.

"You've clearly confused us with two other blokes," he said cheerfully, throwing out the Britishism to be neighborly. "Good-looking guys, probably, but someone else just the same. It being dark and all, I can understand your confusion, but I assure you we weren't meeting anyone here, much less a dead person. We just happened to run across him."

"And you were doing what, exactly, behind a closed restaurant at night?" the slim one wanted to know.

"It's any of your business, I want to know why," Gunn retorted. "In fact, the more you say the more I'm convinced that you're probably the guys who killed him. Seems like we're the ones that should be asking questions, and you're the ones that should be answering."

Both men moved at once, and suddenly there was a glint of metal in their hands. Lorne could barely make out silenced automatics in the dim light. "We'd quite hoped you wouldn't force the issue," the big one declared. "But you leave us no choice. Now, you'll tell us what we want to know or you'll pay the price."

"Well, we ain't talkin', so—" Gunn finished the thought by diving forward and low, at the slender man. A soft thump sounded from the man's pistol, but the shot went over Gunn's head and tore into the metal Dumpster. Gunn tangled himself around the man's legs. Both went down in a heap.

Lorne started to move the instant he realized what Gunn was up to. He knew the big guy—*and thanks so much for leaving me the man-mountain,* he thought—would open fire now that his colleague had. So he lurched to his left, drawing his opponent away from where Gunn and the other one battled. Then he zigged back to the right, and the big man's first bullet whistled harmlessly past him. Before the man could get off a second shot Lorne had scooped up a handful of parking lot gravel and hurled it at his face.

The big man let out a cry and raised a hand to his eyes. Lorne took advantage of his momentary blindness, plowing into his midsection like a linebacker.

Except he wasn't a linebacker, and the guy really was every bit as solid as he looked. Instead of going down, he swung a tree-limb of an arm and batted Lorne to the ground. Then, his sight apparently returning, he aimed his weapon at the scrambling demon and fired again.

Lorne managed to roll toward the man, and the slug chewed tarmac just behind him. Still prone, Lorne spun around and lashed out with a powerful kick that slammed into the man's ankle. The man buckled and Lorne rose up fast, smashing into his wrist with both hands. The gun went sailing.

But the big man wasn't down yet, and even without the weapon he was a formidable opponent. He shifted his weight onto his back leg, the one Lorne hadn't injured, lowered his stance, and sliced the air with his hands in karate-like moves. Lorne found he could almost predict the moves, though, and managed to dodge them. Then when the big man was centering himself for another attack, Lorne moved in again, bringing both hands up high and then together like a cymbal player's, on both of the man's ears. The man staggered under the blow.

"If you can still hear me," he hissed, "I'm a lover, not a fighter. But unprovoked attacks—not to mention murder—sort of raise my hackles. So whatever you get is just what you have coming to you."

The big man just snarled and lunged for Lorne, enraged. Lorne dodged him like a matador, and the man swept past him a few steps, then turned and came again. This gave Lorne an idea. He pranced in front of the man, actually using steps from the Pylean dance of shame. "Missed me, missed me, now you gotta kiss me," he chanted. The big man lowered his head and came again, moving with the force of a hurricane wind.

But Lorne had maneuvered himself close to the restaurant's phony adobe wall, and when he sidestepped, the big man drove his blocky skull directly into it. Adobe crunched and a few chunks skittered to the parking lot's surface. The big man tried to straighten himself, swayed, and tumbled over.

A bullet thudding into the restaurant wall reminded Lorne that there was still another pistol in play. Gunn was grappling with the slim guy, but the man's finger was still on the trigger. Lorne ran to the Dumpster and found an empty bottle of a particularly foul Texas Chianti. *Some places just shouldn't bother producing wine,* he thought as he raised it, waiting for his chance. It came a moment later, and he brought the bottle down across the slender man's head. "Close your eyes, Gunn!" he shouted at the same time, hoping Gunn would have time to react.

The bottle shattered and the man went limp. But across the parking lot, the big one was already regaining his senses, looking for his gun on hands and knees. Lorne helped Gunn to his feet. "Let's make like a banana and get the hell out of here," he said urgently. "The better part of valor, and all that."

"I'm with you," Gunn agreed breathlessly. Together they ran around the restaurant and back to their ride.

When they were sailing down Hollywood Boulevard and the two gunmen were far behind them, Lorne felt the strange low that comes after an adrenaline high dissipates. "Those fellows were tough," he said.

"Got that right," Gunn said with a smile. "Sorry you got the big one, but even the little guy was a match for me."

"That's just because you don't fight dirty enough," Lorne countered. "Or he wasn't stupid enough to run into a wall."

"Either way," Gunn replied.

Lorne remembered the feeling he'd had, that he could predict some of his opponent's moves. "There was something strange, though," he said.

"Stranger than two English guys with guns killing a kid named Camel behind a restaurant with a cartoon chicken for a mascot?"

"It's a rooster, Booster," Lorne replied. "And what was strange was that I knew what the guy was going to do, at times. Like his moves were familiar. We haven't fought those guys before, have we?"

"I think I'd remember," Gunn said. "But you're right, I got the same vibe. But I didn't feel like I'd fought against those guys . . . it was more like I'd fought with them, somehow. Like I felt comfortable with their moves, they were so familiar. See what I'm sayin'?"

"Well, it's dark, so no. But I catch your drift. And if you think about it—two English fellows, a bit on the stuffy side, using moves we felt at home with . . . do you think they're Watchers?"

Gunn agreed. Lorne thought about the many times they'd both fought alongside Wesley, and remembered stories he'd heard from when Wes was younger, trying to be a Watcher to the rebellious Faith, full of himself, stiff and unyielding as an adobe wall.

If there were Watchers in town, and they were shooting people to protect the old man, then something seriously heinous was going down.

ANGEL

Something worse even than they had first believed.
"This is not good at all," he said finally.
"Just what I was thinkin'."

Mission San Alejandro was deserted, its parking lot empty. The silence that enveloped it was broken only by the shrill chirp of crickets and the fluttering of some winged thing overhead. Mildred caught a glimpse of a dark object flying in a zigzag pattern that she believed must have been a bat.

She was glad that the staff seemed to have deserted the place for the night, though she had parked on the street nearby instead of in the lot, just in case there was a security guard or service that would come around. She didn't mind that the mission's main buildings would be locked up tight, because she wasn't especially interested in getting into those. What she wanted was free run of the grounds, and that, she thought, could be arranged even though the place was closed.

As she approached the expansive whitewashed walls she couldn't quite believe she was doing this. For most of her life she hadn't been a particlarly bold sort of person. She had been retiring, a bit of a wallflower, really. She had only met Philip by accident—literally, when he had backed into her car in a crowded parking lot. Under other circumstances she'd never have talked to him, most likely. But he had felt so bad about the accident—and he'd been in the insurance business himself—that he had volunteered to go with her to see her own insurance agent, and he'd helped her fill out the forms, even though he was at fault. During the process of collecting a settlement and getting her car fixed, they had become friends and finally started to have lunches together once a week. Lunches became dinners and the occasional movie or dance. Two years later they were married.

So she wasn't exactly the impulsive type. A lifetime with Philip, more or less, hadn't been a thrill ride, but it had been satisfying and comfortable. Her books took her to exotic locales, and she met danger through the characters she read about, and that was the way she liked it. She wasn't quite sure what had changed now. But something certainly had. Moving toward the mission as silently as she could, hands held out to her sides to help keep her balance in the dark, she had every intention of trespassing on state property in order to help catch a killer.

Philip would never have approved. He'd have pointed to some of his actuarial tables, quoted from a risk/benefit analysis, and sent her home.

I've gone completely insane, she thought, stifling a giggle. *And I love it.*

The massive front doors of the mission were closed up tight, as she expected. But off to one side of the big church building, she remembered, there was an iron fence. She recalled thinking when she had first noticed it that the space between the fence and the church wall was awfully wide—maybe not for most people, but certainly for someone as small as she was. When she reached it now, the space seemed narrower than she remembered. But she'd seen Pookie wriggle through impossibly tight spots, and if her pudgy cat could do it, well, there was no reason that she couldn't.

Mildred put one hand against the cool, rough adobe, and wrapped the other around the upright of the iron fence. She reached one leg through, which was easy enough, and then tried to follow with her body. Thin as she was, though, parts of her were wider than others, and she felt the fence and wall squeeze her in the middle. Her heart began to pound—breaking in was bad enough, but what would become of her if she got stuck here? She eased herself out of the bind, turned her body so she was more parallel to the wall, and tried again. The cold iron bar scraped against her cheek as she slid her head through, but this time her body passed between wall and fence with room to spare.

Not much, she thought. *But a little. Enough that if I have to get out in a hurry I know I can do it.*

Bringing her other leg through, she stood inside the mission grounds, all alone. She'd come this far. It was time to find out exactly what secrets this place kept from her.

CHAPTER FOURTEEN

"I'm so glad you guys are back," Cordy practically shouted as soon as Gunn and Lorne walked through the door. "I'm going nuts trying to find anything about the mystery man online. I mean, you type 'distinguished-looking older gentleman' into a search engine and you get a lot of sad personal ads, but no supernaturally powerful killers. At least, none of these men mention that particular character trait. But lots of them like to take long walks on the beach, especially at sunset. Have you ever really walked on the beach at sunset? You're lucky if you don't step right into some goopy sea anemone or—" She stopped long enough to take a breath. "So, did you find him?"

"No such luck, pumpkin," Lorne answered morosely. "We found some other guys. Maybe just as distinguished-looking, but not quite as old. And they seemed tough enough, but not like the guy you've described. They were more about the hardware and less about the brute strength."

"Are you both okay?" Fred asked, coming down the stairs, her brow furrowed with concern.

"Fine," Gunn said. "But we need to talk to Wesley. He still playin' Paul Bunyan up in the woods?"

"He's still with the Kinrosses," Cordy replied. "If that's what you mean."

Gunn crossed to the phone and lifted the receiver. "You got the number?"

A few moments later he was talking to Wes while Lorne, Cordy, and Fred looked on.

"Watchers?" Wesley asked, surprised by the question. "Are you sure?"

"No, I ain't sure, English. That's why I'm askin' you."

"Well, what made you think they were?"

Gunn took a second to collect his thoughts. He leaned against the edge of a desk, and the hand that wasn't holding the phone gripped the edge of the desk so hard his knuckles were turning pale. He hadn't realized he was quite so tense, but in retrospect guessed that he had been ever since the fight. "They were Brits, like you. Kinda, you know, uptight, mannered. Wearing blazers, dark blue blazers. Who wears a blazer to a murder?"

"They killed someone?" Wesley interrupted.

"This kid we were supposed to meet, who witnessed the old man stealing a car. We're pretty sure they killed him. And they tried to kill us."

"All right," Wes said. "Blazers to a murder sounds a bit odd, but it doesn't suggest Watcher to me, necessarily."

"That's not all of it," Gunn interjected. "When we fought 'em, Lorne and I both recognized some of their moves. It was like fightin' you. Exactly like that. There were some I think of as signature Wes moves, you know—"

"I have signature moves?" He sounded almost proud.

"Of course you do. Anyone you fight with, long enough, you know what kinds of punches they'll throw, how they block, when they'll try a kick or something else. And these guys—they coulda been you, way they fought."

"I see." Wesley was quiet for a moment, mulling. "I can see how that would suggest Watcher training. Still, I don't think that they were Watchers."

"But it's possible."

"Anything is possible, Gunn. But Watchers aren't usually quite so ruthless as you're describing. Killing a young human, for instance, isn't exactly their style. Trying to kill you and Lorne, on the other hand . . ."

"Hey, we're on the side of the angels. Well, the Angel."

"I know that, but they would see a demon and his human accomplice. Anyway, as I was about to say, I doubt that it's Watchers for another reason. Word on the grapevine is that there's been some serious attrition in the ranks—some kind of organized campaign against Watchers. There are precious few left, if any, and I doubt that any who are still alive would be loitering around Hollywood."

"Then who else could these guys be?" Gunn asked him.

"A couple of possibilities come to mind. But given what you told me about their combat techniques and their general ruthlessness, I'd guess they were Scholars."

"They were pretty old to be in school."

"No, Gunn. 'Scholars' with a capital *S*," Wesley clarified. "There's an organization called the Scholars of the Infinite. They broke off from the Watchers Council hundreds of years ago. But one of the Watchers who split away from the Council to help form the Scholars was Henry Millbank, who was the primary combat trainer for the Watchers in those days. He developed most of their combat techniques. Watchers still learn the Millbank system, and Scholars do as well."

"Could be these guys, then," Gunn agreed. "If the Millbank system means they fight like you do."

"It would mean that, yes."

"So how many of these secret organizations are there?" Gunn wanted to know. "This is startin' to sound like those signs you see in small towns, you know? Jaycees, Optimists, Lion's Club, 4-H, and oh yeah, Watchers and Scholars of the whatever."

"Scholars of the Infinite," Wes said again. "They believed the Watchers were a bit too—how shall I put this? Namby-pamby. Putting all of their enforcement efforts behind Slayers, who, as you know, tend to be teenage girls. Very powerful teenage girls, but still. The Scholars thought the Watchers themselves should take a more active role in battling the forces of darkness, and when the Watchers refused, the Scholars broke away. They exceed the Watchers in the depth of their dedication to the study of the supernatural, and far exceed the Watchers in the level of brutality to which they'll stoop. They're totally dedicated to secrecy and to the importance of their mission, and they'll stop at nothing to see that they can carry it out."

"So killin' some innocent civilians . . . no big thing?"

"If they believed the civilians were a threat to their mission, or might somehow expose their workings? No big thing at all. The end, to their minds, justifies the means. Battling evil will save lives in the long run, even if it costs a few from time to time."

"Great," Gunn said. He put his hand over the mouthpiece and addressed those gathered around him. "Wes says we got a big problem on our hands."

"Who's there?" he heard Wesley ask.

"It's me, Cordy, Fred, and Lorne," Gunn told him. "Angel's out someplace."

"Checking on the stolen truck, I think," Fred said.

"Someone should look in one of my books—I'm pretty sure it's there, in the hotel."

"Check a book," Gunn relayed. "What's it called?" Wesley had a lot of books.

"*A Brief History of the Infinite,*" Wesley responded. "Volume eleven, I believe."

"Out of how many?"

"Thirty-two," Wes said.

"That's brief? I'd hate to see the unabridged."

"It's a library in Blackburn."

"Did you leave a word out of that sentence?" Gunn asked. "Or did you say it *is* a library?"

"It's a fairly extensive history," Wesley explained. "And it's not a public library. I had a glimpse of it once, but you have to be a Scholar to have access."

"Okay, hang on." Gunn covered the mouthpiece again, out of habit—he didn't really care if Wes heard what he was saying. "We need to check out a book called *A Brief History of the Infinite*. Volume eleven." Into the phone, he added, "What are we lookin' for in this book, Wes?"

"Now that you brought up the Scholars, or the possible Scholars, at any rate, I have a vague memory of some Scholar activity in this part of the country.

Centuries ago, mind you. But look for any mention of the Spanish missions, or Mission San Alejandro in particular. And I might be wrong about the volume number. Without looking myself I can't be sure. So check the surrounding volumes as well, if you don't find anything in that one. It may shed some light on what's been happening around here."

"Got it," Gunn said. "How're things out in the woods? Peaceful? Any Princess Charmings come to kiss Sleeping Ranger?"

"No princesses," Wes assured him. "But things are . . . lively. I'd better go."

"All right," Gunn said. "Stay sharp."

"You do as well," Wes said, and broke the connection.

Gunn hung up the phone and they all went to Wesley's books—those that Wesley hadn't come back to claim at one time or another, at least. That still left a large number of volumes to work with, including, Gunn learned, the entire thirty-two book *Brief History*. The books were leather-bound, each about an inch thick, with gilt embossing that had chipped and worn off over time. "We're looking for any references to the California missions," Gunn told the others, "or Mission San Alejandro. Wes thinks there's some kind of connection between this Watchers Council splinter group, the Scholars of the Infinite, and whatever's goin' down out at the mission."

Each took a volume, Gunn number nine, Fred ten, Cordelia eleven, and Lorne twelve, and they sat down in comfortable chairs to thumb through them. "It's too bad there's no index," Lorne said. "You'd think scholars would want them to be more user-friendly."

"Yeah," Cordelia agreed. "They could put all this on CD-Rom and have a search function."

"I get the idea these Scholars are more interested in keeping secrets than sharin' 'em," Gunn told him. "To the point of being willing to kill for it."

"So he thinks those nice polite fellows who tried to kill us . . . ?"

Gunn nodded. "Scholars, not Watchers."

"Didn't seem very scholarly to me," Lorne pointed out. "But then, my experience with higher education is pretty much limited to betting on the Fighting Irish from time to time."

"They ever win for you?" Gunn asked.

"Come to think of it, no. But I like green."

"Will you two pipe down?" Cordy demanded. "Some of us are trying to read here."

Gunn and Lorne shared a look, and they both turned back to their books.

Twenty minutes later Cordy let out a whoop.

"You scared me," Fred complained. "Did you find something?"

"Only the jackpot," Cordelia said with a broad

smile. "Listen up—and I'll paraphrase, since whoever wrote this must have been paid by the word."

"Got that right," Gunn put in. "I never read so much extraneous crap in my life."

Fred shot him a stern look. "Let's listen to Cordelia."

He mimed zipping his lip and looked expectantly at Cordy, who was studying the page. It was volume eleven after all, Gunn noted. Of course, if he told Wes that it'd just make him even more insufferable, so he planned to keep quiet about it.

"If I can understand this lame version of English correctly—King's English, my butt—," Cordy said, "the whole mess started in 1779. A padre—they call him Fray Obregon in the book, kind of went nutso at, ta daa, Mission San Alejandro. He stopped focusing on his mission duties—which included lots of praying and overseeing the mission Indians who were supposed to be getting educated, but also lots of time working in the mission fields and milking the mission goats and so on—and instead started experimenting with the occult. Always a bad sign. Should I stop editorializing?"

"Take your time," Lorne said sharply. "It's not like there are people dying."

Cordy gave him a sheepish glance. "Yeah, sorry," she said. She went on, but more to the point. According to what she described, Fray Obregon began tampering with occult forces and quickly slipped over the edge of sanity. He told those who tried to question him that he had always had magickal powers, but had learned that he could amass more by performing certain rituals. Each California mission had two padres assigned to it, and a group of soldiers, but he was the one in charge at San Alejandro, and even though the other priest and some of the soldiers questioned his newfound interest, none of them felt they could stand up to him or stop him. When the second priest finally tried, Obregon cut out his heart and fed it to a mongrel dog he kept. The soldiers gave up on trying to rein him in at that point, and deserted in the night. Obregon was left alone with several hundred mission Indians.

But Obregon had always had strong supporters among the Indians. He had learned early to play members of different tribes off against one another, and he did that now. As his ultimate ritual he arranged for the sacrifice of a hundred Indians. They were impaled on stakes and raised high on the mission grounds, and he walked among them, bathing in their blood and soaking in their death cries, firmly believing that he would be granted the ultimate power that he sought.

When the soldiers reached Monterey with their stories of Obregon's madness, word rapidly spread to Spain and then to the pope. The Scholars of the Infinite had spies close to Pius VI, so they heard about Obregon almost as soon as he did. Pius took the matter seriously enough to send some agents to the New World to deal with Obregon. But the Scholars had already detected a massive power field emanating from that area and knew the pope's representatives would find themselves outmatched. So they sent some Scholars over as well.

They confronted Obregon, who by then had turned San Alejandro into his own personal fiefdom, ruling through terror and relying on the small army of well-armed Indians who had stayed faithful to him to help keep the rest in line. The former mission had become a kind of hell on earth, with instruments of pain and torture taking the place of the sacred artifacts that had once been commonplace. Demons had the run of the grounds, but Indians who committed the slightest transgression might find themselves drawn and quartered, sometimes after watching the same happen to members of their families. Alone the pope's agents were powerless, but the Scholars joined in the battle, and together the two groups fought a terrible mystical battle with Obregon. The Scholars and the papal agents were ultimately successful. Unable to destroy Obregon, they incarcerated him and were able to separate him from most of his power, which was confined within a particular casket.

Obregon himself was taken to a special underground prison in Trealaw, in southern Wales. Here he was kept in solitary confinement, in a cell that was enchanted to keep his remaining powers muted. Over the years his jailers aged and died, but he never did—he remained the same age, and never became sick. Nor did he ever repent his crimes. The casket, according to the book, was long since lost.

"So this Obregon is in Wales," Gunn said, "in jail. I see how the Mission San Alejandro is connected, but how is Obregon?"

"The book is at least a hundred years old," Fred pointed out. "He was imprisoned when it was written. But what if he's out? What if he escaped and came back? That's something that would bring the Scholars out of the woodwork, isn't it?"

"You're right, peanut," Lorne said. "From what you said about the Scholars, Charles, they're real big on maintaining secrecy. If this bad boy broke out, they'd want to recollar him in a hurry, before he could cause any trouble and blow their cover."

"And he'd have a reason to come back to San Alejandro," Cordelia added, "if he thought he could reclaim his power there." She shivered, and not from the cold, Gunn thought. He had some goosebumps himself. "I think we need to call Angel," Cordy said. "He needs to know what's going on."

Do they really think that yellow tape is going to keep anyone out? Angel wondered. The warehouse

Fred had told him about was sealed with yellow police crime-scene tape. Also, the door was locked. Neither barrier presented a problem to Angel, though. The two cops sitting in a squad car outside were marginally more of a difficulty, but even they weren't impossible to get past. Angel simply went around to the side of the warehouse, where a window twenty feet off the ground had already been broken, probably by a kid with a rock and maybe a slingshot. He jumped, got a grip on the windowsill, and broke out enough glass to slip inside. Then it was an easy drop to the floor.

Except that the floor was buried under about two feet of trash. Virtually the entire space was a sea of refuse, except for a corner that had been cleared out—blood stains on the floor confirmed for Angel that it was where the warehouse owner's body had been found. A path from there to the door had been created by the removal of the body, disturbing the evidence, and Angel was pretty sure that when crime scene investigators showed up in the morning to go through the rest of this stuff, they'd be unhappy that Angel had been there too. But then, they'd be unhappy about this whole scene, which would probably take days to process. Angel had never seen so many bits of trash in one place. Particularly trash that had once been a good-size truck.

He'd seen the old man shred a tire with one

hand, and he'd felt the man's strength when they fought. So he knew the guy was strong. But this—tearing an eighteen-wheeler apart with what looked like his bare hands and strewing the pieces around—he was pretty sure that was a feat that was beyond his own capabilities. Which made him nervous. *What if the old guy can take me?* he wondered. *What if he can rip me to pieces like he did this truck?*

The guy must have been furious, Angel speculated. He didn't do this much damage just because he was looking for something. There were no pieces left bigger than a refrigerator door. Angel's guess was that he'd taken the truck, looking for something specific among the mission's artifacts. Not finding it, he had turned to the truck itself, thinking it might be hidden somewhere on it. Still thwarted, he had simply gone berserk, tearing the truck into tiny pieces. He saw bits of sheet metal, pieces of the bench seat, wires, instruments from the dashboard, strips of tire, wooden objects that could only have been the mission's furnishings, all torn apart. If he had found what he was looking for at any point, Angel believed, he'd have given up his destructive rampage and left something whole. But he didn't stop until everything in the huge space was reduced to its smallest bits.

That was all the place had to tell him, though. Maybe it could tell seasoned forensic scientists more, but Angel didn't have days to sift through the pieces looking for fingerprints or traces of DNA. Probably the old man had cut his hands ripping sheet metal with them, and there would be blood stains about that wouldn't belong to the warehouse owner or the dead trucker. But Angel doubted the crime scene techs would be able to connect that DNA to anyone. This place was helpful only in that it gave Angel another indication of his opponent's strength.

He was about to leave, via the same window, when his cell phone rang. *I should remember to put it on vibrate when I'm trespassing,* he thought as he fished it from his pocket and thumbed the button to answer it.

Fifteen minutes later Cordelia had told him about the murderous Scholars in town and given him the capsule version of the Obregon story. "Looks like I need to go to the mission," Angel suggested.

"Angel, this guy Obregon, if that's who it is—he's tough."

"I'm tough too. And if the book's right, he's had most of his power taken away from him."

"Still . . ."

"One more thing, Cordy. I'm no Scholar."

If Mildred Finster believed in such things, she'd have suspected that the mission grounds were haunted. Illuminated only by a moon that kept slipping behind cloud banks, the white walls of the buildings were silvery and sinister, the shadows sharp-edged and deep. Anything could be hiding in those black spaces. To reach the buildings from where she had entered the grounds she had to walk through a graveyard, where ancient priests and mission personnel were buried, and the shifting moonlight made the low stones seem to move about on their own. Night-blooming flowers scented the air, reminding her of a funeral home she'd visited several months before. A couple of bats flitted above her, the beat of their wings leathery and disturbing. When she crossed the broad plaza she felt very exposed.

Worse, she felt as if she were experiencing things that just couldn't be—like there was another reality, separate from her own, on the other side of a very thin veil. In that world solemn men walked in long rows, shoulders hunched, wooden poles in their hands, while others stung their backs with lashes. Women sat in pools of blood and keened their anguish. Fires licked at smoke-blackened walls and engulfed the abandoned toys of children. Mildred could almost, but not quite, hear peals of maniacal laughter and the ripping sound of sharp blades tearing flesh. She shuddered at the tricks her own imagination played on her and forced her attention back to the world she knew.

Her destination was the back corner of the mission, where tourists weren't allowed and things were still in disarray. Furnishings being brought to the mission, she reasoned, were almost certainly intended for this section, since she'd looked at the established tourist zones and they were already furnished in a historically accurate fashion. So if some object on the truck had been the killer's target, it had been something meant to go into the area under renovation. She wasn't sure what she could learn about the place at night, but in the daytime, with rangers and workers about, she would certainly learn nothing at all.

Now, with no one around to chase her away, she went to the doorways and narrow window slots leading into the rooms still being refurbished. Drawing a small flashlight from her purse, she shone its beam into the rooms as far as it would reach. The floors of these rooms were dirt, but level, the walls adobe that had been scrubbed clean and in some cases whitewashed. There were no cobwebs; clearly the rooms in this section had been prepared for the furnishings.

When this proved unhelpful, she went to where the caution tape sealed off the breezeway. She flashed her light down the breezeway, confirming that it was empty; it was very dark inside and she had a bad feeling about it. But after that glance she started along its cool length, holding her hand out to touch the wall with every step, just to keep her bearings. In a few moments she reached the other end, where the separate outbuildings stood, clearly limned by moonlight. These, she had noticed before, were farther back in the renovation schedule, and she wanted a closer look at them.

She was approaching the nearest one, her flashlight clutched in a fist that trembled a little in spite of her best efforts, when she heard a new sound. Kind of a rustling in the dirt. A rat, maybe, or some other night creature, like a raccoon or opossum. Or, she worried, a skunk. They all were active on southern California nights. She aimed the flashlight in the direction from which the sound had come, keeping its beam close to the ground, expecting a pair of beady eyes to come into view.

Instead she saw a pair of feet in leather walking shoes. Dark pants above those. Higher still, a fist holding what seemed to be a gigantic pistol, which was aimed directly at her.

"Save your batteries," a man's voice said. Her flashlight beam had stopped at the gun, so she still hadn't seen his face. "You might need them where you're going."

CHAPTER FIFTEEN

"I just thought you'd want to know," Cordelia told him. "Since you're up there and your books are . . . y'know, not."

"Thank you, Cordelia," Wesley said. Much of what she'd told him about the Scholars in America and their struggle with Obregon sounded familiar, now that she'd reminded him of it. Every Watcher knew bits and pieces of Scholar history, just as every executive at Pepsi no doubt paid attention to what went on at Coca-Cola. "I have heard some of that. And of course, every Watcher knows of the Scholar prison facility in Trealaw. That's coal-mining country. The prison is actually cut from the bedrock surrounding one of the old mines—a barred door, constantly guarded, is on one side, and hundreds of feet of solid stone are on the other three."

"Sounds tough to get out of," Cordelia replied.

"Quite. But then your friend Obregon is no ordinary prisoner. If I remember correctly, as you say, his power was contained in a special casket, and kept well away from him. Not only that, but the key to the casket was sent in yet another direction, so even if Obregon were somehow reunited with the casket, he wouldn't be able to open it and reclaim his power."

"So you do agree the old guy we've been running across is most likely him?"

Wesley paused, looking across the room at Madelyn Kinross, who sat working on a crossword puzzle in the light from a floor lamp. If it was Obregon who came here, she was indeed lucky that Angel had been on the scene. "It sounds as if it probably is, Cordy," he said. "Which means you've got to be very careful, all of you. He'll be no one to take chances with. If he's back here, back at the mission, then it must mean he's figured out a way to regain his power. Or at least that's what he's trying to do. Either way, he's very dangerous."

"We kind of had that figured out already," Cordelia reminded him.

"Yes, well . . . if he does get his hands on that casket and that key, he'll be beyond dangerous. It took a unique combination of magickal forces to put Obregon away before, and even then they couldn't manage to destroy him or eliminate his power. They could only just manage to contain it. I suspect the Scholars are just as tough as they've ever been, but somehow I doubt that the Vatican's forces are as practiced as they once were."

"We'll be careful, Wes. You too, okay?"

"You can count on it," he assured her. "Keep me posted if anything else happens."

When he hung up the phone, Madelyn Kinross was staring at him, her crossword magazine abandoned in her lap. "Is something wrong?" he asked her.

"Did... did you say something about Obregon?" she queried, her words halting and hesitant.

"I did," Wesley confirmed. "Do you know the name?"

"I... I think so. Let me look at something." Madelyn went into the room in which her husband slept, and Wes followed her to the door, curious. She opened a closet door and rummaged through the contents of an interior shelf. In a few moments she emerged with a blue wirebound notebook in her hand. Holding it toward Wesley like a prize, she said, "This was the last of Gene's journals, before..." She glanced toward the still form on the bed. "Before that. He used to write every night, just jotting notes about the day, what birds or animals he'd seen, funny stories that happened at work, or whatever. After he went to sleep, I filed them in here, in chronological order. I kept thinking that some day he'd wake up, and they might help him remember how things were . . . you know, before."

"And you think he wrote about Obregon in there?"

Madelyn shrugged. "The name sounded really familiar when I heard you say it on the phone," she said. "I couldn't imagine why—it certainly isn't the kind of name one hears very often. So when you said it, it jogged something in me. I think Gene mentioned it, on one of his last good days. If he did—and if it was important, or noteworthy, he'd have put it down in here."

"May I see?" Wes asked, extending a hand toward the notebook. She held it back for a moment, as if making a decision, but then handed it to him.

"Probably better that you read it," she agreed. "There are . . . too many memories in there for me. I haven't read it since that first week. You'll find some of the words are smeared, I'm afraid." She smiled forlornly at him. "Tears. Silly, huh?"

"Not at all," Wesley assured her. She went back out to her chair and her crossword, and Wes sat down with the journals of a man who had effectively vanished from the earth thirty years before, even though he was just in the next room.

"The state parks system is going to be the death of me yet," Wesley read after scanning pages long enough to find pertinent passages. Gene Kinross's handwriting was neat and fluid, though, as Madelyn had warned, the pages were sometimes blurred and streaked.

We've spent months cataloguing, packing, and shipping junk that's been gathering dust and cobwebs here for decades, hundreds of years, sending it all into storage near Sacto. But at the same time—bless bureaucracies everywhere—they're sending us stuff from a renovation job in Arcata, things they swear originated here. And sure enough, the first box I opened checks out against Obregon's original inventory list. The stuff belongs here, but the timing stinks. We're trying to make enough room to get started on some major reconstruction projects of our own. Budgets kept going up and down, projects kept getting approved and then delayed, but we were finally making some progress, and had cleared out space to work, and the state headquarters starts sending us new stuff that has to be checked in, organized, cleaned, and stored somewhere. It's gotten so bad I'm seeing boxes in my dreams at night, and I don't know if they're coming or going.

One thing today was strange. We've all heard the legend of Obregon, of course—the mad monk who slaughtered natives all over the mission grounds, finally had to be taken out by an army of the pope's, or something like that. Most employees here dismiss it as a bunch of ghost stories, totally unbelievable nonsense. I'm not so quick. I'm a rational guy and everything, but I've seen things around there, especially at night. And heard them. Cries that sound like Gabrielino Indian languages, to my untrained ears—and Gabrielinos in incredible pain, at that. One night I swore I could see flames, and in the glow of the fires, the silhouettes of stakes with bodies twitching and writhing on them. Then I blinked and rubbed my eyes, and it was just headlights from a car taking the corner sweeping across the wall. So am I crazy, or are the ones who dismiss the stories crazy? Or both?

But one thing that I found in one of the Arcata shipments reminds me of the stories. In one of the shipments there's a big box, like a small casket, hand-carved from mahogany, it looks like. Roger came across it first and couldn't open it for anything. He let me take a crack at it, but same thing. No way in, and there's no keyhole or anything. All there is on the front is a little cutaway section, in a shape like a little sunburst. The cutaway doesn't go inside the box; it's just like a space where some decorative inlay fell out, maybe.

A chill ran up Wesley's spine. Gene Kinross had, he believed, found the casket in which Obregon's power was contained, though hundreds of years after Obregon had been stripped of it. He kept reading.

Anyway, the box got put away someplace—I

didn't put it anywhere, and Roger swears he didn't either, but someone did because when I looked for it later I couldn't find it. The reason I looked for it is that I found, inside a different box that I was able to get open, a little sunburst emblem. It looked like a piece of hammered copper, on a rotted leather thong like it was worn as a medallion. As soon as I saw it I thought it would fit in that space on the first box. But I couldn't find the box to check for sure.

The other strange thing is that neither of these items, the mahogany box or the little sun emblem, are on Obregon's inventory. But everything else in this shipment is. I don't know what it means. I brought the emblem home with me to study further. Maybe I'll take it into L.A. to see if one of the antiquities profs at UC can shed any light.

Wesley was surprised to turn the page and see that the next couple of pages were blank. But he flipped a few more, and saw that Gene Kinross had picked the journal up one more time. The handwriting had lost its neatness, though—here it was rushed, half script and half jagged block printing. *Sentence fragments, half-thoughts . . . ,* Wesley noted. *It looks like something written by a man on the verge of madness, or at least blind panic.*

Strange things are going on here. Cold inside, so cold. Maddie out at the movies with Beth-Anne. Good thing, too—too scary here right now. The noise of shutters banging at the windows. But our shutters are down for the summer, out in the garage. High, moaning winds outside, but when I look out all's calm. In here I can see my breath; fingers cramping from the cold, and the stove's broken or something, not putting out a bit of heat.

Another possibility too . . . it's all in my head and I'm cracking up.

Seems likeliest, in fact. Head throbbing with pain. Not a migraine—100 times worse. I can barely hold the pen and I see . . . winged things coming at the windows and hear the wailing of the dead and . . .

Wesley flipped more pages, but that was all Gene Kinross had put down. He closed the book. Madelyn was looking at him, her face sad but somehow resigned to her sorrow, after all this time.

"That's the last thing he wrote," she said. "He came home with that thing, that medallion or whatever."

"The sunburst emblem," Wesley supplied.

"That's right. He showed it to me. I went to a movie with a friend. I shouldn't have left, I knew—he'd come home early that day, not feeling well; he said he'd had a bad headache at work most of that afternoon. But he seemed okay. When I left he was in bed, starting to write about the day, about the emblem. When I came back he was on the bedroom floor, that notebook lying next to him. There was no sign that anyone had been here, no sign of any strange weather. The stove wasn't lit—it was a perfectly lovely fall evening, still warm. The doctors think he had some kind of seizure, maybe a tumor or something like that, giving him hallucinations before the coma set in. But then they could never find any sign of a tumor or any other physiological problem, so...."

"But that's because there wasn't any," Wesley said with certainty. "It was not in his mind at all. It never was."

"What do you think, all that's real? That this is somehow related to that little sunburst thing, or whatever?"

"Certainly you've seen enough that's beyond what is considered 'normal' experience, or perception, not to discount that," Wesley said.

"I've seen some very strange things," Madelyn admitted.

"Was your husband crazy?"

"He was the sanest man I ever knew," she said, with absolute conviction.

"Then there's only one answer left. And I believe you know it's the truth. There's more to this whole tale—the story of Obregon is literally true, and your husband came into contact with both the box in which Obregon's power was stored and the key—the sunburst emblem—to open it. The combination of those items was enough to stir mystical

ANGEL

forces, making Gene some kind of nexus of powers and putting him into a coma which you yourself admit that medical science can't explain."

"I don't know the whole Obregon story," she said. "Just what little I heard from Gene, or read in his journal, and what I heard you saying on the phone. But—"

"That emblem is here, in the house, isn't it?" Wesley interrupted, speaking with sudden urgency as the truth became clear to him. "That's why the supernatural activity has increased here in the past few days—because Obregon is back in town, and his proximity to the box and the key is upsetting the supernatural balance again. If he finds them both, if he can get that box open—what you've seen so far will be only the barest hint of how bad things will be. And not just here, but everywhere."

"It's here," she said. "I haven't seen it in decades, but I kept everything from Gene's last days, just in case." She looked down, shamefaced, at the magazine in her lap. "I know I shouldn't have kept it, it's not our property. But . . ."

"It's all right," Wesley said, trying to sound reassuring but fully aware that he was only barely succeeding, if that. He felt that finding the emblem was the highest possible priority. "Probably better that it was here rather than at the mission. If it hadn't been kept away from the box all these years,

God only knows what might have happened. Is it in the closet, where the journal was?"

"I don't know," Madelyn said. She rose, hands twitching, reflecting Wesley's own anxiety. "I'm sure I put it somewhere. But I thought it was just a trinket, you know?"

"Yes, I understand," Wes told her. She headed back to Gene's room, Wesley right behind her.

"That was so long ago," she said, opening the closet. This time he pushed in beside her, taking a look for himself. There were four shelves inside, filled with notebooks, manila envelopes, and boxes of every size and description—the detritus of a life on hold. "It could be anywhere in here, or it could be somewhere else altogether."

"It's vital that we find it," Wesley said. "I can get it someplace safe, get it into Angel's hands."

"That would be good," Madelyn agreed as she pawed through the closet's contents. "Maybe . . . maybe it'll help Gene, if we get it away from him."

Wesley wasn't so sure. "Perhaps," he said. He didn't want to dash her hopes, but saw no reason to encourage them either. Keeping the emblem away from the box was the important thing. In the greater scheme of things, what happened to Gene Kinross hardly mattered. "Is there someplace else I can look while you're—"

"It's here!" She pulled a worn white business envelope from inside a shirt box on the second shelf. "I remember now, putting it in this." Prying open the envelope's flap, she shook the emblem out into Wesley's open palm. It was, as Gene Kinross had described, nothing much to look at. About two inches in diameter, it was little more than a flat disk with rays radiating out from its center. There was a little bit of relief to it, but not much—a circle around the middle that indicated the sun, and some wavy lines in the rays. The back, where it was meant to lie in the box's cutaway space, was flat. At the top a hole had been punched for the thong, but there was no thong with it now.

"Hard to believe this little thing could be the cause of so much trouble, isn't it?" Madelyn asked him. She sounded almost as if she wanted him to reassure her that it wasn't. He could hardly blame her—she wouldn't want to think she had been harboring the source of her husband's difficulties for all this time.

"It isn't just this," Wesley reminded her. "It's what this represents—what it can do. I'll call Angel—we've got to get this to him right away."

He started for the phone, but heard a car scraping gravel outside. Had Angel come on his own? Wesley looked out the window.

But it wasn't Angel. In the light that spilled through the window, Wes saw an elderly-looking man in a cream-colored suit—*Most unseasonal*, Wesley thought absurdly—walking toward the house.

"That's him!" Madelyn gasped with obvious horror. She stood at his shoulder, looking out at the visitor.

"Obregon?"

"If you say so. That's the man who fought with Angel."

"Don't worry," Wes said. "There's a protective spell around the house. If he's a magickal being, he won't be able to get past it."

As they watched, Obregon swaggered toward the cabin, his gaze fixed on the door, completely ignoring the two people staring at him from the window. He took a few steps forward and then stopped, as if he'd run into an invisible barrier of some kind. Which was, Wesley knew, exactly what he had done. His mouth turned down in an angry scowl, and Wesley felt his spirits start to rise.

But then Obregon tore at the barrier, his hands encountering momentary resistance but then ripping through the barrier as if it were nothing more substantial than cotton candy. He stormed up the steps to the front door. The momentary optimism Wesley had felt was dashed to the floor. A second later the door crashed open and Obregon swept inside.

"Where is it?" he demanded. His voice roared like a freight train at full blast, much louder and more forcefully than one would expect from a man of his size and apparent age. But his stance and demeanor matched his roar—he looked powerful and fierce, not aged and decrepit. He stood in the entryway like he owned the place and meant to tear it down, and Wesley felt a shiver of fear. He could hear Madelyn behind him, panicky noises coming from her throat.

"There's nothing for you here," Wesley stated, hoping he sounded as certain as he was trying to. "Just go."

Obregon turned slowly to face him. Wes could barely believe that he was so afraid of such an old man wearing a ridiculous suit. "Where is it?" the man said again. This time his voice was lower but still carried all the menace of a mad dog.

"I don't know what you're talking about," Wesley said.

"The key."

"There's no key here. Except possibly to the door you just broke." *Again,* he thought, remembering that Angel had already broken it once.

"Bring me the key," Obregon insisted. He held his stance, legs spread for balance, and raised one hand, palm up. "Bring it now."

"Oh, let's just give it to him," Madelyn said, breaking into sobs so that she couldn't even get the last word out.

"No!" Wesley shot back. "You won't get it, Obregon. Go before I have to take matters into my own hands."

"You?" Obregon permitted himself a sly smile. "And just what would you do to me? Sweat on me? Soil my suit? The lady has the right idea, little man. Let her give it to me."

"The lady was mistaken," Wesley insisted, "since we've nothing to give you." Wishing that Emil had finished with his spring-loaded sleeve blade, he reached down for the enchanted dagger he wore strapped to his ankle and raised it toward the man.

Obregon shrugged. Wesley had never seen a simple shrug so laden with peril. "I suppose you've made your choice?"

"I have."

"Then there's nothing for it," Obregon said. Wes anticipated the move but wasn't fast enough to dodge it. Before he could even fully brace himself Obregon had sprung from his wide-footed stance and rammed his fists into Wesley's midsection. The ex-Watcher doubled over, gasping for breath. He tried to get a slash at Obregon with the dagger, but the old man simply hoisted him into the air and hurled him into the next room. Wes slammed into a wood-paneled wall, bounced, and hit a table, upending it. The dagger flew out of his hand. He saw bright flashes of light, like flashbulbs going off, and when he tried to right himself the world went dark.

Some indeterminate period of time later, Wesley opened his eyes and there was light again, though there was also spinning, as if he'd ridden a carousel for far too long. He reached out for one of the several pieces of furniture that seemed to be scattered about him, but it didn't support his weight and he crashed to the floor again. He tasted blood, his ears were ringing so loudly he thought someone had stapled a telephone to his head, and when he tried to breathe, an agonizing pain lanced through his chest. *A cracked rib*, he guessed. *Lucky I'm still alive, I suppose.*

When he opened his eyes again, Madelyn Kinross was there, helping him to a sitting position. "Do you need an ambulance?" she asked. She'd been crying—her eyes were red and puffy, and she kept sniffling. "I should have called one but I was afraid."

"I'll . . . I'll be fine," he said, wincing at the pain. "Is he . . . gone?"

"He's gone," she told him. She looked away, toward the ceiling, the wall, anyplace but at him. "I . . . I gave it to him. To make him go away. I gave him the sunburst."

Wesley wanted to scream at her, but breathing that deeply hurt far too much.

"I know I shouldn't have. But I just wanted him to leave. And he did, he left, right away."

Wesley shook his head. "I'm afraid he's only out of our hair momentarily," he said, trying to work the slightly bent blade back up his sleeve so he didn't cut himself. "You didn't mean to, I know. You couldn't have fought him anyway. But I'm afraid you've doomed us. You've doomed all of us."

CHAPTER SIXTEEN

The man led Mildred into the small, run-down outbuilding. He allowed her to use her flashlight to illuminate her path, as long as she kept its beam directed toward the ground. He came behind her, and she was hyperaware of the big gun in his meaty hand. She was certain it remained pointed right at her.

She was equally certain that if she entered that building she would never come out alive.

But no other good option presented itself. If she tried to run she wouldn't get more than a few paces, especially in the dark, before he would be on her. If he chose to use the gun he wouldn't even have to give chase—he could simply shoot her before she had made any progress at all. The same went for screaming—he could silence or kill her within a heartbeat, and there was no guarantee at all that anyone was within earshot.

So she went where she was told, even though when the black doorway gaped before her, panic welled up and threatened to overtake her. She swallowed it down, fighting for breath, willing her legs to take another step, then another. At the doorway she paused, gripping the jamb for dear life.

"Inside," the man said, his voice a hushed growl.

"There is definitely a very large misunderstanding here," Mildred said desperately.

"Save it," he replied. "I've seen you snooping around here before."

Oh, my, she thought fearfully. She had felt certain she'd been unobserved that time. *Maybe I'm not quite the sleuth I believed myself to be.*

Summoning her last reserves of courage, she stepped through the doorway into the building. The air inside was close and dusty. She hesitated inside but felt the man's hot breath on the back of her neck. "Keep going," he instructed. She obeyed, and as she went farther into the building she saw a hatchway in the floor, open wide, with a worn, wooden staircase leading down and out of sight.

"Oh," she said. "Surely you don't want me to go down there?"

"In there," he confirmed.

"I'm not good with stairs and ladders," she told him, fearful of what his response might be. "You might have noticed I'm not exactly spry."

He didn't surprise her. "It doesn't matter to me if you fall or climb, lady."

Then I'll just have to do my best, she thought. Her only chance was to stay alive as long as possible, in hopes that something would happen to give her a chance to survive.

She just didn't know what that something might be.

So she went along with him, shining her light down the hole in the floor—its weak beam didn't even reach the bottom—and then turning around and backing onto the stairway's top step. It wasn't really a ladder, despite her protestations, but a primitive wooden stairway, its steps worn smooth with the passage of years and feet. Her feet had a hard time finding any traction on them.

All the way down into the dank, cool earth, Mildred bit her lower lip to keep from sobbing out loud. She didn't know what she had stumbled into here, but she had no reason to expect this man to show her any patience or mercy whatsoever. If she started to cry—which, more than anything, was what she wanted to do right now—she felt sure he would have no problem putting a bullet into her head. She couldn't even imagine what Miss Marple would have done in similar circumstances—all her fictional detectives had abandoned her now, leaving her alone with ugly reality.

After descending what she felt must have been

twelve or fifteen feet into the ground, she once again felt solid earth beneath her feet. She backed away from the staircase and turned as quickly as she could, playing her flashlight's beam before her. She had come down, it seemed, into some kind of underground chamber, and it looked as if the man had been staying down here for a while. She saw a flat area with a sleeping bag unrolled on it, a large ice chest, a propane stove, and a couple of battery-powered lanterns. Other supplies were tucked here and there about the room, which smelled mildewed and unclean.

The man rumbled quickly down the staircase behind her. "Have a seat," he told her when he had reached bottom. "We could be here awhile."

She flashed her light around again. "Have a seat where?" There were no chairs to be had.

"Anywhere you want," he replied simply. "Except the bed. That's mine."

If you can call that a bed, Mildred thought. Sitting on the floor for very long would wreak havoc with her back, she knew. But there didn't seem to be much choice. She moved close to a wall and used it to help lower herself to the ground. The man turned on one of the lanterns and sat cross-legged on his "bed," gun resting in his lap. He didn't speak to her any more, and Mildred took advantage of the opportunity to study him a little. He was a big man, weighing at least twice what she did, with broad shoulders and a flat, dull face. His clothes looked like those a person half his age would wear—he looked to be at least in his mid-forties, and yet he wore a football jersey and ridiculous baggy pants that ended just below his knees.

I should have run, she thought. *If he tried to chase me his pants would have wound up around his ankles and he'd have tripped.*

Of course, there was always the part where he might just have shot her.

"Are you keeping me here for some specific reason?" she asked him after a while.

"My orders are to hold on to any snoopers," he told her. "My . . . employers will be along in a while. They'll want to see you."

"Surely you can tell that I'm no danger to whatever it is you're doing here. I'm just an old woman."

"You're a nosy old woman," he retorted. "With a flashlight. And you broke into the mission after hours. You aren't as innocent as you act."

"I was just a little confused," she attempted. "My cat got loose and I thought maybe he came here."

"Uh-huh," the man said. "You can shut up anytime. You're staying here till they come, no matter what you say." He turned away from Mildred and stared at some spot on the wall over her head. She didn't see any sign of reading material, or a TV or radio or anything like that. She wondered, if he had been there as long as it seemed, what he did to entertain himself. She had never quite trusted people who didn't read. Even Pookie . . . well, he didn't exactly read, but if she had a book or a newspaper open on the table he would almost invariably park himself right on top of it, as if he expected to absorb the words through osmosis.

She wished now that she had brought along a book, because her captor was plainly in no mood for conversation and she was not at all interested in staring at the wall for hours on end.

The good part was that they didn't have long to wait. But the bad part was that when the man's employers did come, they were also armed. They dressed better than their employee, though, and their English accents were almost charming. The first one down was slender with distinguished-looking silver hair and wild eyebrows that looked like some creature that Pookie might find and bring home after a hunting expedition. The other man was huge, so tall that he had to bend over to keep from bashing his head on the chamber's ceiling.

"What've you got for us then, Graham?" the slim one asked.

The man who had brought her in pointed at her from his seated position. "Her, Mr. Atkins. Saw her poking around here yesterday, and now she's back."

"Hardly seems threatening," the larger one commented. "Bit on the scrawny side, isn't she?"

"You didn't tell me to weigh anyone, Mr. Dodds," the man they called Graham countered. "You just said to keep an eye out for anyone paying more attention than they should. That's what she was doing, and I've seen her here before, too. She's here in the middle of the night, practically, nosing around with a flashlight—she's got to be up to something."

"Well, madam, Graham may not be tremendously articulate, but he makes a good point," the man called Mr. Atkins said to her. With his accent and his gentle voice he sounded almost reasonable. "What have you got to say for yourself?"

"I'm not sure why I should tell you anything," Mildred protested. She worked her way up to a standing position, again using the wall to help her. "He . . . he pointed a gun at me and forced me into this . . . this awful pit. That's kidnapping, at the very least. That's a federal offense in this country, you know."

"We've committed far worse," Mr. Atkins told her with a sinister smile.

"Well, you needn't act so proud of it," Mildred rejoined. "I'd be ashamed if I were you. Terrorizing innocent people like this. And for what?"

"Oh, very definitely for good reason," Mr. Atkins replied. "I daresay even you might not object so strenuously if you knew what we were up to."

"Why don't you tell me, then?" Mildred inquired.

"I don't think you're in a position to be making demands," Mr. Dodds snarled at her.

Mr. Atkins wagged a long, slender index finger at his larger compatriot. "Now, now, Mr. Dodds," he said. "The lady's point is well taken. We have, shall we say, deprived her of her rights, to some extent. And I don't know about you but I don't get the sense that she's a tool of Obregon, do you?"

"He's a tricky one, though," Mr. Dodds pointed out.

"I certainly am not a tool," Mildred insisted. She didn't know who this Obregon person was, but she was very sure that if she were a tool of anyone she would know about it.

"And it's wonderful to hear you say so," Mr. Atkins assured her. "Though you'll understand, I hope, if we can't simply accept your word. Obregon is, as Mr. Dodds says, a bit trickier than that."

"I don't even know Obregon," Mildred shot back. This whole situation had her dander up, and that was a fact. Her joints were beginning to ache and she had decided that she didn't like having guns pointed at her even one little bit.

"Obregon is evil personified," Mr. Atkins explained. "If you don't know him, I'm sure your life is the better for it. I, sadly, have met him on two occasions previously, and neither will go down in memory as good days." He glanced about the cramped chamber. "Couldn't you have brought some chairs down here, Graham?"

"I don't mind the floor," Graham answered.

"It's hardly ideal for entertaining visitors, though."

"Don't get a lot of those, either."

Mr. Atkins snickered at that. "With these accommodations, one can see why. Mr. Dodds, please help the lady down."

"I don't need to sit," Mildred snapped at him before Dodds could come near her. "And if I change my mind I'm perfectly capable of doing it by myself."

"Very well, then," Mr. Atkins said. "But I trust you don't mind if I do?"

"I'm not the one with the gun," Mildred observed.

"Quite right," Mr. Atkins said. He helped himself to a spot on the floor. Graham was sent back up to the surface to continue standing guard. Mr. Dodds leaned against the far wall, his hands stuffed into his blazer pockets as if trying to rip it apart at the shoulders. Mildred could no longer see any weapons, but she knew that both men were armed, and even if they hadn't been, she couldn't hope to overpower them.

"The first time I met Obregon he was, of course, in Trealaw, in southern Wales." Mr. Atkins seemed to be talking only to Mr. Dodds, not to her, since he wasn't explaining much. But she had the sense that the audience wasn't necessarily important—

he had a story he wanted to tell, and it didn't matter who heard it. "Some prisoners, of course, are put into solitary confinement if they're particularly ill-behaved or a danger to others, but Obregon may be the only one on earth just now who is the only prisoner of an entire facility. The prison at Trealaw has a couple of dozen cells, I'd reckon, but the others are left empty, and anyone the Scholars need to incarcerate goes to one of the other facilities scattered about the Isles. Trealaw's is built into the side of a hill, an imposing fortress of a place made from native stone, with most of its walls the hillside itself. This night, rain came down in sheets as we drove up the hill toward it, and my first real glimpse of the place—and I realize just how much like a low-budget horror film this sounds—was when a bolt of lightning split the darkness and showed me what looked like an unnatural growth on the hillside."

"You've already lost me," Mildred interjected. "I don't know what scholars you're talking about, and I still don't know who Obregon is."

Mr. Atkins was silent while she spoke, but then continued as if she hadn't said a thing. She decided her first impression had been right. He would tell what he wanted to tell, and interruptions would not be appreciated.

"The front gate of the facility opened as we drove up, and we were able to park the car inside, under the overhang of the entryway. Still, the wind was driving the rain and we—my escort, Mr. Smiggs, and I—got pelted as we dashed for the prison's front door. We were met there by Mr. Freed, the chief administrator, who had spent half his life as Obregon's jailer and who was, perhaps, a trifle unbalanced as a result."

"I met Mr. Freed once," Mr. Dodds said. "At an Annual—the one time he felt he could attend safely. Seemed a nice enough sort, but you're right—a bit odd. Started at the slightest unexpected noise."

"I remember that," Mr. Atkins added. "That was the year that Obregon killed two guards who let their defenses slip while Mr. Freed was away. He never left the grounds again."

"That's right," Mr. Dodds agreed with a grin. Mildred had the strangest sensation that she was listening in on two strangers discussing their high school reunion. "I'd forgotten that part. Mostly I remember Mr. Freed jumping half out of his knickers when a waiter dropped a tray of glassware after the banquet."

"That's the man," Mr. Atkins said. "Talked a mile a minute, he did, as if he got so lonely when there weren't visitors that he saved all his words up for any who did drop in. He met us at the door and jabbered at us for a while, then escorted us into the cell block." The man's eyes met Mildred's now; it was the first time since beginning this story that he'd actually acknowledged her presence. "You've probably never been to such a place, ma'am, and Lord willing you'll never have to. Makes this mission feel positively modern. As I said, the building was constructed of local rock. Trealaw's in a coal-mining district and the rock there was almost as black as coal. The facility had been modernized; they had electricity, indoor plumbing, and so on, but it was all put in well after the original construction so it ran in pipes and conduits bolted to the walls and ceilings. The corridors themselves were narrow and cold and the electric light bulbs could barely illuminate such a barren, dark place. Traveling down those corridors felt very much like walking backward in time, into the very depths of antiquity.

"And, as Mr. Freed pointed out which cells had been occupied by which prisoners, most of whose names I recognized as the worst sorts of criminals on earth, the depths of depravity as well.

"Finally we reached Obregon's cell. There had been armed guards, of course, at various checkpoints along the way, a locked door behind each one. At the last door, four guards were stationed at all times, and the door had a triple-lock system. Two of those guards accompanied us through the doors and into the last corridor, which was as dark and frigid as the rest but which, filled with the essence of Obregon, felt somehow more horrible still. The air inside was a veritable miasma of evil; I felt I could barely get enough clean oxygen out of it to fill my lungs."

Mildred was fascinated by his story now. She still didn't know who Obregon was, how this had anything to do with her, or why it resulted in that man Graham aiming a gun at her. She wished for her comfortable chair, and possibly Pookie. And a cup of hot tea wouldn't be a bad thing just now. But for the moment she was content to let Mr. Atkins continue his narrative.

"This was a few years before the time Mr. Freed came to the Annual," he went on. "But security was tight, just the same. I had been sent by the Scholars Review Board—and no member has this duty more than once—to pay the yearly visit to Obregon to see if he was yet prepared to renounce his crimes." Mr. Atkins allowed himself a quick smile. "Merely a formality, of course. No one actually expects him to agree. But I did my duty. I stood on the other side of the bars from Obregon. I looked at my piece of paper, rather than at him—his countenance, I'm not ashamed to admit, was terrifying to me—and read the words printed on it with a voice that I'm sure quavered a bit with the fear that coursed through me. When I was finished reading the whole thing I lowered the paper and forced myself to regard him while I waited for his answer."

"And what did he say?" Mr. Dodds asked. He seemed just as caught up in the tale as Mildred was.

"I've never seen a more terrifying sight," Mr. Atkins said, not exactly answering the question. "He just looked like a man, of course. Aged, healthy—you might think he resembled a favorite uncle, perhaps, or a grandfather. His hair was thick and silver, his eyes small but clear. He smiled at me. 'Come closer,' he said. I didn't move, of course—I was well out of his reach, and if he'd tried to grab through the bars the guards had strict orders to beat him back. But then he said it again. 'Come closer.' His voice, little more than a whisper, had a hypnotic quality to it, and in spite of myself I took a step toward him. Mr. Smiggs and Mr. Freed both grabbed my arms and held me back. Obregon fairly beamed at my obvious discomfort, and then he spoke again. 'Yes, that's good,' he said. There was the very faintest whistle to his voice, particularly pronounced when he made an *s* noise. 'I can see you quite clearly now.'

"I realized that I had been standing in the shadows, but had moved into the circle of light that escaped from his cell. He hadn't meant to attack me—though he probably would not have hesitated if he'd had the opportunity—he just wanted a better view of me. But then he went on speaking. 'You look like someone else I met once,' he said. 'You can't be the same man, though, because I sliced a line all the way around his head and peeled the skin off it, like an orange. Slowly, of course, reviving him whenever he fainted. He lived through most of it. His pain was simply delicious.'

"That was all I needed to hear, of course, to know what his official response was to my question. I marked the form I had brought, and Mr. Smiggs, Mr. Freed, and I hurried away from him. Mr. Freed wanted us to stay the night, but Mr. Smiggs and I had no interest whatsoever in that idea. We raced back to Trealaw and found a room at a guest house there. I didn't realize just how much I had been affected by my brief encounter with evil until the next day. Driving back to London, I had the wheel and Mr. Smiggs was sleeping next to me. At one point he whistled as he snored and the sound of it brought the full memory of Obregon back to me in a horrible flash, as if it were Obregon and not Mr. Smiggs sitting beside me. I panicked, lost control of the car, and ran into a lorry going toward Trealaw. Mr. Smiggs was unharmed, but I broke a leg. The lorry driver tried to avoid our car, though, and his rig tipped over, killing him. Turned out he'd been driving fresh linens to the prison facility. I never have got over the belief that somehow Obregon caused the accident himself, just to unnerve me. And I haven't driven a car since, have I, Mr. Dodds?"

"Not that I've seen, Mr. Atkins."

"That sounds like an awful thing," Mildred said. "And this Obregon sounds like a terrible man."

"In every sense of the word 'terrible,'" Mr. Atkins replied. "If you do not, in fact, know him, then you are indeed fortunate. Let's hope you don't have the chance."

"How would I?" she asked. "If he's in this prison you described."

"Ah, but he's not," Mr. Atkins revealed. "He's here, in Los Angeles, right now. This is why Graham has detained you. We have every reason to believe that Obregon is on his way here, to this mission. There are . . . objects here, which he wants. Our goal was to find him and stop him before he made it back here, but so far, I'm sorry to say, we haven't managed that. We hired Graham to keep an eye on things here, to make sure he didn't slip in without our knowledge. And, of course, to stay alert for anyone else who might be doing Obregon's bidding."

"You said you met him twice," she reminded Mr. Atkins, intrigued now in spite of herself. "What was the other time?"

Surprised, Mildred thought that Mr. Atkins crimsoned at the question. "Oh, that," he replied hastily. "I was on the review panel after an unpleasantness when . . . well, when Mr. Freed somehow fell under Obregon's sway and served up the tongues of several of the guards to him, like canapés on a silver tray. When he realized what he'd done, he blew his own brains out. There was, of course, an investigation. Several of us questioned Obregon together, and when he saw me he refused to answer any questions unless I was the one asking. And he refused to call me by any name other than 'orange.' The whole thing was most embarrassing, and of course entirely unsatisfactory."

Mildred could see that Mr. Atkins didn't like talking about that occasion, and offered him a way out. Anyway, that was ancient history, as far as she was concerned, and there were more pressing matters at hand. "But why would he be here?"

"Because this is the seat of his power," Mr. Atkins explained. "I won't go into all the details—I feel like I've dominated the conversation quite enough already—but it was here that he gained his power, and here that he was stripped of it. But he couldn't be killed, nor could his power be dissipated. So it was locked away into a kind of casket, which was shipped far away from him and from the key. Now the casket and the key are both back in the area, and their proximity to one another set off what you might think of as a psychic earthquake, powerful enough to be felt even in Trealaw. As a side effect Obregon's powers were heightened sufficiently to enable him to escape, killing more than a dozen guards and Scholars in the process. We didn't know where he had gone but we knew where he would come. So here we are."

"Because Obregon is coming here, to the mission? And you think that the two of you can stop him even if he gets the key and the casket again?"

"We had hoped to find him before that happened," Mr. Atkins admitted. "If we fail, then I'm not sure there's a force in the world strong enough to stop him."

Much about this story was still confusing to Mildred, but she figured she could work her way through it. Certainly it bore little resemblance to the mysteries she read; though at the bookstore she had seen some with supernatural elements, they had never sounded appealing to her. But if this man's story wasn't purely a delusion—and if it was, it seemed he and Mr. Dodds shared the same one—then her beliefs would need to change, to a very great extent. She thought she could make the necessary shift. It was, after all, nothing more than a puzzle, she realized—a real-life puzzle, with potentially enormous consequences. But a puzzle just the same, and she was good at puzzles. "You talk like you're the good guys," she said. "So why kidnap me? Why commit what you yourself said were far worse crimes?"

This time, the taciturn Mr. Dodds spoke up. "You ever heard of the Scholars of the Infinite, mum?"

Mildred shook her head. "No, I can't say that I have."

"That's the way we like it to be. If it became known that we exist, it would make our job harder. And if it became known because of something like this—because we let Obregon escape—then it could be the end of the Scholars. While you don't know about it, the Scholars have spent the last several hundred years helping to keep the world safe from all manner of evils. So it's important to us to keep it secret."

"Exactly," Mr. Atkins said. From underneath his blazer he drew a wicked-looking black pistol. "Which means we can't allow any witnesses to survive."

Mildred swallowed down her fright. His accent might have been thick, but Mr. Atkins's meaning was crystal clear.

The guy with the gun was easy; candy from a baby. He skulked in the shadows, where human eyes might not have seen him, but Angel wasn't human. He could see the man clearly, could smell the oil and gunpowder of his weapon as well as something else—a powdery scent he recognized as that of Mildred Finster.

He worked his way behind the armed man and came up to him silently. At the last moment he reached out and tapped the guy on the shoulder.

The man started and spun around, and Angel laid him flat with a single punch. The guy's head bounced off the wall behind him, and he fell into Angel's arms. Angel lowered him silently to the ground, then took his gun and emptied it before snapping off the trigger.

So Mildred Finster was here somewhere, and had been close enough to the armed thug to leave a trace of her scent behind on him. *But where is she now?* he wondered. *And more importantly, who else is around?*

There was more going on here than was readily apparent, he could tell. The atmosphere seemed electric, charged with magickal forces. It unnerved him a little, and he could sense that he would have a fight on his hands soon enough. But first things first—he needed to find out what had happened to Mildred. He couldn't see any indications of a struggle anywhere nearby, so he relied on another of his preternaturally sharp senses, and he tried to follow the path that Mildred had taken. Other odors mingled with hers—sharper and more recent ones, sweat and cologne—but they all seemed to lead Angel in the same direction. He sniffed his way to what seemed to be an empty building, but the odors were even stronger inside, and in the dark he could clearly see an open hatchway leading down.

And from inside the opening he heard voices.

One of them belonged to Mildred. He didn't recognize the other, but the intent of the speaker was clear. Angel didn't bother with the ladder but simply stepped into the opening and dropped, his black duster fluttering like leathery wings.

He landed with a thump, knees slightly bent, but immediately straightened and turned to size up the situation. Two men were there with Mildred, and the smaller of them had a gun in his fist. "Drop it!" Angel commanded.

Instead the man fired it.

The slug slammed into Angel's chest, hot and hard, and he took a step back. Mildred screamed, the sound echoing in the tiny space. Angel shook his head and moved toward the gunman, who fired twice more. These two, at even closer range, drove Angel to his knees.

"Mr. Angel!" he heard Mildred wail.

Instead of answering her, he forced himself to his feet again and charged the man with the gun. Before the guy could get off any more shots Angel was on him, squeezing the wrist of his gun hand and clutching at his throat.

"I'd drop it," Angel hissed between clenched teeth, "because if you don't you're going to lose the hand."

The bigger man, Angel knew, was on the move— he was too large, and the room too tiny, for him to travel quietly. Both of these guys were human, he knew, and he could take them—but Mildred couldn't, so if the big man went for her instead of Angel it would be a problem.

He didn't.

Still holding the small man, who struggled and clawed at Angel with his free hand but didn't drop the gun, Angel started to turn, but the big guy shoved a gun against the back of his neck.

"What are you?" he asked. "Vampire? You must be the Angel we've heard so much about. Let's see if you can shake this off so easily."

Angel knew a shot at that range, in that area, would do serious damage. He could survive it—the man was right, he was a vampire, and they didn't kill easily. But it would put him out of action long enough for them to get away with Mildred Finster.

Not gonna happen, he thought.

Simultaneously he ducked his head forward away from the gun, lifted the smaller man off his feet, and spun. The small guy whipped through the air like a kid on a carnival ride, and Angel swung him into the bigger man. They collided hard. The big man staggered and his gun went off harmlessly, the bullet driving into the earthen ceiling. The smaller guy let out a moan, and Angel realized he'd broken the man's arm when he spun him.

Well, he shot me, Angel thought. *So we're even.*

Angel threw the smaller man against the wall. The big one was still standing, though, and he still held his gun. He pointed it at Angel. Angel didn't much like guns to begin with, and in the last few minutes he'd had to deal with three of them.

"Look," he said, trying to sound reasonable, "you know that's not going to work on me. Either you've got a stake or you don't. Since you're still holding that gun, I'm guessing you don't. So you either put it away, or I take it from you. Which one do you think is going to hurt less?"

The big man's face screwed up as he thought it over. He glanced at his friend, unconscious in the corner, then back at Angel. After another moment he shook his head. "This is too important," he said. He moved the gun away from Angel and aimed it at Mildred, who cowered, terrified, against a wall.

That was all Angel needed to prompt his next move. He dove at the man, faster than any human could follow, and smashed him back against the wall. With one hand he caught the man's gun wrist and whipped it down, bringing his own knee up to meet it. Bone crunched and the gun spun from the man's hand. The big guy tried to use his other hand to attack but Angel head-butted him; then Angel released the broken arm and used both hands in concert, just as he had on the speed bag earlier. The big man's eyes glazed over, and when he fell Angel dodged his bulk as he would a falling tree.

When the room was still again, Angel turned to Mildred. "Are you okay?"

She shook with fear as she regarded him. "You're a . . . a . . ." She couldn't bring herself to finish the sentence.

Angel knew that she had already seen too much to deny it. "I'm a vampire, yes. If I hadn't been, I'd be dead and you'd still be their prisoner. Remember, I'm on your side."

She couldn't control her quivering, though. Angel felt bad for her. She had brought this on herself, he knew, but she hadn't understood when she started just what she was letting herself in for.

"But . . . but you . . . and those men . . ."

"Who are they?" Angel wanted to know.

"They're . . . I think he said Scholars. Scholars of the Infinite. They're after someone named . . . named Obregon."

"Oh," Angel said simply. He shrugged. *Too late now.* "Well, then, I guess they're on our side too. But they were going to kill you," he reminded her.

Talking seemed to help calm her down, but it was obvious that she'd need a lot of calming. "I knew too much," she said, her voice still breaking. "It's . . . an old story."

"Do you know why they're here?" Angel asked her. "Why they were holding you?"

"I think they just wanted to make sure I wasn't working for him," she said. "And then, because I'd found out about them, they were going to kill me."

"Is he here yet?" Angel queried. "Obregon?"

"I don't know," she said. "I haven't seen him, and they hadn't either."

"I sensed something, outside," Angel told her. "Something powerful, and dark."

"That could be him, then," she agreed. "From what Mr. Atkins said, 'powerful' and 'dark' are certainly two words that would apply."

"I need to find him, then."

"Before he finds the casket and the key, if he hasn't already."

He looked at the old woman with surprise as he helped her toward the ladder. "You know a lot about this," he observed.

"And I think I know where we should look," she said, smiling for the first time since he'd arrived. It was a nervous, slightly terrified smile, but a smile just the same. She started up the wooden staircase, but stopped to meet his gaze. "But we'd better hurry."

CHAPTER SEVENTEEN

Mortified at his defeat by Obregon—*"Defeat" is hardly the word for it,* he thought, *unless modified perhaps by "crushing," or "humiliating"*—Wesley knew that very little time remained in which to set things right again. He tried calling Angel's cell phone but there was no answer. The vampire could have it turned off, but more likely he had let the battery drain or simply forgot it. Next he rang the Hyperion, but got only an answering machine.

That's it then, he thought. *Once again, I'm on my own. And this time facing a more powerful foe than I ever have.* He reclaimed his enchanted blade, not that it had done him much good, while Madelyn Kinross wept quietly on her sofa.

I shouldn't have been so harsh with her, Wesley realized. *It wasn't her fault that Obregon got the key. I'm the one who was sent here to stop him, not her.* But he had already apologized for his outburst, and it had done no good. She continued to blame herself, and that, coming on the heels of decades of pain and sorrow with what seemed very few bright spots, had thrown her into a deep funk. Wesley hoped that she emerged, if not right away, then tomorrow or next month or next year.

He hoped there was a world around into which she could emerge by then. From what he knew of Obregon's potential power, the world of tomorrow might scarcely resemble that of today.

He was nearly ready to leave when he heard a sound from the other room. At first he thought he'd imagined it, or that it was, perhaps, a night bird on the windowsill or an animal outside. But then he heard it again—a rustling noise, followed by what seemed like a low moan.

"Mrs. Kinross," Wesley whispered.

She was already on her feet. She shot him a glance and ran into her husband's room with Wes on her heels.

Gene Kinross had raised himself up on his elbows and looked toward the doorway in surprise. He blinked a few times, like a man waking up from a long nap. "Maddie?" he asked, sounding confused. "Is that you?"

"Oh, Gene," she said, rushing to him. She threw her arms around him, tugged him to her bosom. "Gene, you're back."

"Maddie?" he asked again, pulling away slightly.

"What's the matter? Are you . . . you look so old. And who's that?"

She stared at him, in shock, and then her tears began to flow again. *Of course she looks old to him,* Wesley thought. *She's aged thirty years while he slept.*

And he knew something else as well. The timing of Gene Kinross's awakening was no coincidence. The proximity of the key was what had kept him asleep, and the magickal aura that surrounded it was responsible for the events that had terrorized his poor wife. Now the key was gone, taken by Obregon, so of course Gene was awake again. Awake—and the one person around who might be able to help Wesley stop Obregon's plans.

"Mr. Kinross, listen closely to me. You've been asleep—comatose, essentially—for a very long time. You're fine now, and you'll have plenty of time to get caught up, to reestablish your connection with your wife, who loves you very much and has cared for you all these years, but—"

"Years?" Gene interrupted. "What are you talking about, years?"

"Please, sir," Wesley urged. "This is very important. You remember the legend of Obregon, don't you? The key, the casket? You brought the key home."

"Yes, of course," Gene said. "That was . . . well, yesterday, it feels like. But—"

"Obregon is back," Wesley cut in. "He's taken the key, and he's gone to get the casket. If he does, then we're all in grave danger. You, your wife, the very world we live in. I can't overstate the possibilities."

"I don't even know who you are," Gene said. "Or what you're doing here with my wife. And Maddie..."

"My name is Wesley Wyndam-Pryce," Wes told him. There wasn't time to let him ask the questions. "Madelyn can vouch for me. Right now I need you to help me find the casket, before Obregon does. I can try to fill you in more on the way, but I'm afraid it's going to take quite a bit of time before all your questions are answered."

Gene rubbed his eyes with one hand and looked from Madelyn to Wesley and back again, his disbelief showing on every inch of his face. "I just . . . *years*? How is that possible?"

"Like I said," Wesley repeated, "I can tell you more on the way. We need to go, now—or else I do. But I don't know where Obregon would look for the casket, so it would be a great help if you would join me. If you can walk, that is."

"I feel fine," Gene said. He swung his legs off the bed, planted his feet on the floor, and put his weight on them. "A little hungry, I guess. But fine."

"It's been a . . . a while since you've eaten, honey," Madelyn said between her sobs. "I'll make a nice dinner and we can catch up. But I think Mr.

Wyndam-Pryce is right—it's important that you go with him now." She swallowed hard and went to the closet to fetch him some clothes.

Gene Kinross looked completely lost. Wesley sympathized. His wife was thirty years older than he remembered her. He couldn't help feeling confused by what his body told him—which was that he had only been asleep for a little while, maybe just a single night—and by what he was hearing, not only from his suddenly aged wife but from an utter stranger making bizarre demands of him. But he was also, Wes realized, a man who liked to help, whose career choice had been based on a willingness to work hard for comparatively little financial reward in the service of the public good. Since to him, not much time had passed, he was still effectively that same man, and it didn't take him long to make up his mind.

"If it's true that Obregon has the key—hell, if it's true that he even exists—I guess we have to stop him if we can," Gene said after a moment's contemplation. "I was never completely sure he wasn't just a ghost story, though I was being somewhat convinced by what we'd found." He took the pants Madelyn handed him and stepped into one leg. "Let's get going, pal, and you can bring me up to speed on the way. Just answer me one question before we go."

"Certainly," Wesley agreed. "What is it?"

"You two say I've been out for years, right? So what year is it?"

Wesley told him. The man's already pale face blanched even further. "That's not even the century I remember," he said, staggered by the idea. "Are we going to the mission in some kind of flying rocket car?"

A hot, dry wind whipped the mission grounds, shaking the trees and kicking around bits of debris left behind by the day's tourists. Southern California was known for its moderate climate, but when the sun went down the nights were usually cool, not balmy, so the wind felt odd to Gunn. He noticed a sharp ozone scent to the air as well. "I don't like this," he said quietly, clutching his ax handle with extra force. "Something ain't right here."

"I don't mean to be disagreeable, Charles," Fred countered. "But if things were 'right' here we probably wouldn't have bothered to come."

She had a point. "S'pose that's true."

"I know what you mean, dumpling," Lorne chimed in. "There's definitely a sinister vibe in the atmosphere. If the padres hadn't already passed on I'd be surprised if this didn't chase them away. I've got that shivery spine deal going on myself."

They had driven out to the mission after Cordy had last talked to Angel. He was on his way here, she had said, and he'd need backup. Wesley was

ANGEL

busy at the ranger's house, standing guard, so it was just Fred, Lorne, Cordy, and himself. At night, in the dark, the mission seemed much larger than he remembered, and he wasn't sure how they were going to find Angel. Short of calling his name, which seemed like a supremely bad idea. They walked as quietly as they could, scouting the grounds with mini flashlights. At Fred's suggestion they had spread out far enough that they could still see and speak to one another, but could cover more territory than if they all walked together. Each carried at least one weapon, and Gunn had an unpleasant feeling that they might be needed before the night was over.

On the ride out Cordy had filled them in on what Wesley had told her about their quarry. None of what she said made Gunn feel better about the idea of confronting him. But there was still hope that he could be defeated if he hadn't yet found the box his power was stored in and the key to open it. Right now that was foremost in Gunn's mind. He didn't want to see any of his friends die, and there was every indication that Obregon, with his power restored, might just be too tough for them.

After they had scouted for a while, he heard Fred give a low whistle. "You guys!" she called softly. "Over here!"

She had been on the outside edge of the wide-spaced group, heading up the walkway and shining her light into the various rooms they passed. But now she beamed it down a breezeway, facing away from the main plaza. She beckoned them with a waggle of her hand, and the three of them dashed over to her.

"Look," she said, her voice an exaggerated whisper. She played the flashlight against the base of an outbuilding's wall. Gunn heard Cordy's gasp of surprise when she saw what Fred had spotted.

"Who is that?" she asked.

"I'm thinking past tense might be more appropriate," Lorne countered. "Who *was* that?" He might have had a point there. Up against the wall was a man's body, still and twisted at an awkward angle.

"You think he's dead?" Fred asked, worry creeping into her voice.

"He ain't dead; he's gonna be powerful sore when he wakes up," Gunn speculated. "Probably wish he was."

"We should have a closer look," Fred suggested. "Either Angel did that, or Obregon did."

"Or someone else," Lorne pointed out.

"Because that's what we need," Cordelia replied. "More players to worry about."

They slipped beneath tape that was supposed to keep the tourists out of the breezeway and walked toward the unmoving man on the other side. When they emerged on the outside of the main mission compound, the air felt even more highly charged, as if they'd walked into some kind of freakish electrical storm. Gunn felt the hairs on his arms and the back of his neck standing straight up. "There's some weird stuff goin' on here tonight," he whispered, mostly to himself.

But Lorne was close enough to hear him. "You can say that again, brother."

Moving around to the other side of the building, more than happy to keep his distance from the possibly dead guy, Gunn noticed that a soft glow emanated from within the building. He hurried to the doorway and looked inside. Light splashed up from an opening in the floor. "You guys," he said. "Might want to check this."

He felt Fred come up behind him—sensed her, he supposed, because her scent, the sound of her breathing, and the rustle her clothes made when she moved were so familiar. "Are you okay, Charles?"

Gunn realized he wasn't quite sure how to answer. His normal response would have been full of bravado, even if it hadn't been entirely real. But somehow that didn't seem appropriate right now. He wasn't sure if it was the strange atmospheric conditions, or if the whole Obregon story just disturbed him more than usual for some reason, or what. But he felt an unease that was rare for him, and not at all pleasant.

Obviously Fred had noticed it as well.

"I'm fine," he said, after a moment. "Just a little freaked I guess."

"I've got your back," she assured him. "We all do."

He chuckled without humor. "Guess that means I go in first, huh?"

"Unless you want me to."

Of all the things he did want, that was just about at the bottom of the list. "No, I will." He hefted the ax and walked into the single-roomed building, toward the glowing, gaping hole. He heard the others filing in through the doorway behind him.

Before he peered over the edge into the chasm below, he lowered himself quietly to his knees and listened. No sound at all. After a long moment he poked his head over the side, then drew it back again quickly. He had seen what looked like a man's leg down there. But when the man attached to it didn't shout out or shoot anything at him, he looked again. It was a leg the size of some tree trunks he'd seen, and it hadn't moved. He moved his head so he could see the rest of the guy, and, like the one outside, this one had definitely had better days. His face was bruised and pulpy; his clothes, which looked more dressy than was absolutely necessary for the occasion, were torn and disheveled. It was a few seconds before Gunn realized he'd seen the man before, only considerably less beaten up.

"Lorne," he hissed. "Check it! That's that guy

from the restaurant. Those two English dudes, remember?"

Lorne leaned over the hole and murmured his agreement. "Looks like he had an accident."

"I'm bettin' it was on purpose," Gunn riposted. "Anyone else smell the hand of Angel here?"

"Maybe without so much of the metaphor mixing," Lorne said. "But that could be tall, dark, and fangsome's handiwork."

"There is a staircase," Cordelia pointed out.

"Yeah, I see it," Gunn said. He hadn't been anxious to go down, but he guessed someone had to. At least he didn't need a flashlight. Keeping a firm grip on the ax, he descended cautiously. Once he was down, though, he decided that his worries had been groundless.

"Lorne," he called up. "Both those English guys are down here. Both out cold."

"Warms the cockles of my Pylean heart," Lorne responded.

Gunn took a quick look around the rest of the space. It was a small room carved from the earth, with a few belongings that made it look as if someone was living here, at least temporarily. A battery-operated lantern glowed steadily, which was the source of the light that had drawn him. At first he thought there was nothing else to see here, but then he noticed something that seemed out of place—a white clutch purse on the floor, leaning against one of the walls. He was sure he'd seen that purse before.

Mildred Finster had one.

He was about to shout out again when he heard some kind of commotion above him. *Great,* he thought, *Obregon's come and I'm down here instead of up there where I belong.* He raced to the stairway and lunged up it as quickly as he could—just in time to see Wesley and a pale guy in a ranger's shirt and faded jeans coming into the little building.

"Hello, Charles," Wesley said. "This is Gene Kinross. Ranger Gene Kinross. He might be able to help us here."

"Gene Kinross, the mattress tester?" Gunn asked, trying to cover his shock. He glanced at the others and saw that they all wore the same stunned expression he was hoping he wasn't. Guy had been in a coma for thirty years and now he was standing there with Wes. Gunn had seen a lot of strange things in the last several years, and this was right up there with the strangest. "I hope somebody can help," he admitted. "Because I got a feeling Mildred Finster is here somewhere, and maybe in trouble. I found her purse downstairs."

Kinross nodded. "I know where she might be, then," he said. Gunn started to emerge from the hole but the ranger waved him back down. "Stay," he said. "We're joining you."

"There ain't a lot of room down here," Gunn told him.

"We won't be there long," Gene Kinross answered. "It's just a way station."

"Way where?" Gunn inquired. "Only the one door I can see."

"But that doesn't mean there isn't another one," the ranger said. "Let me show you."

Gunn dropped back to the floor and backed away from the stairs, keeping an eye on the two unconscious British men. What had Wes called them, Scholars of the Infinite? Looked more like they were studying the insides of their eyelids right now.

The ranger came down, followed by the rest of the group, with Wesley bringing up the rear. Gunn had been right: The room was crowded now, especially with sleeping Scholars sucking up the floor space. The ranger stepped lightly over the slumbering forms of the Scholars and went to the wall farthest away from the stairs. "I don't know if this is the path they'll have taken," he said as he did so. "But it's the most direct route to where I think they'll be going." He put his face close to the earthen wall, as if looking for something tiny there. After a few moments he must have found it, because he inserted the tips of two fingers into holes that Gunn would have sworn were just natural features. With that as a grip, he tugged, and a counterweighted door swung open, as smooth and easily as if its hinges had been lubricated just that day. On the other side of it was a dark opening—a square tunnel about five feet across.

The ranger turned to the others with a smile. "They built these places to last," he said. "Let's go." Then he was swallowed up by the darkness of the tunnel.

CHAPTER EIGHTEEN

The sky crackled and roared like something alive, hot and angry as a wildfire consuming dry tinder. Heat lightning rumbled across the heavens in a fantastic rainbow of colors: red, violet, bright orange, pure white, cerulean blue. Ferocious winds tore at rooftops, scattering lawn furniture and forcing the foolhardy few who ventured out to take refuge inside houses or cars. Loose shutters—or those loosened by the gale—banged like strangers desperate for shelter, but those who owned homes near the mission had no choice but to turn up their TVs or stereos, hunker down, and wait for the storm to blow over. Even then, when the winds snagged power lines and tipped them down, sparking and flailing across the streets, electricity failed and those appliances became nothing more than useless boxes.

This was no natural storm, and it would take more than a shift in the jet stream to end it.

A dozen feet under the earth, Angel could still hear the punishing winds above. Mildred had led him to the mission's sealed off "old" section where, she had come to believe, Obregon would most likely seek the casket that confined his powers. After searching the closed rooms for a few minutes he had found the entrance to what seemed to be a warren of ancient tunnels, dry and cool, running underneath the mission grounds. He wanted nothing more than to leave her someplace safe so he could explore alone, but until he knew where Obregon was—and that there were no other Scholars around, or their employees— there was no place safer than with him.

The tunnels were dark, which wasn't a problem for him, but Mildred had left her flashlight back in the room where Angel had found her. As a result she kept stumbling on the uneven floors and either falling into rough-sided walls or into Angel himself, slowing his progress. He knew time was critical, so now and again he debated simply abandoning her to speed his search.

But before he decided to do so, he heard distant laughter echoing down the tunnels. "That's him," he whispered.

"What?" Mildred asked, sounding confused. "I didn't hear anything."

ANGEL

"Quiet," Angel warned. He heard more now, footsteps, he thought. They seemed to come from a side branch of the main tunnel he and Mildred were in. "Stay behind me," he whispered as they turned the corner.

A dozen yards down this side tunnel Angel saw an open doorway with flickering light showing through it. Cobwebs had blocked it completely, but something had torn through them and now they hung like tattered curtains in the uneven light. "Oh," Mildred said quietly when she saw it.

Angel clamped a hand over her mouth and put his face close to hers. "Don't make a sound."

She nodded her understanding and he released her, turning his attention back to the glowing doorway. In absolute silence he covered the distance in seconds and stopped just outside. Then he placed his fingers at the edge of the door for balance and peeked in.

The room had been, it seemed, a torture chamber of some kind. Angel knew at a glance that the casket hadn't been stored here—not if it had been sent away and only recently returned to the mission. Judging from the thick layers of dust and massive webbing covering the room, no one had been here in decades at least, except for the man who now stood with his back to the door. The man was admiring a carved wooden casket about half the size of an ordinary coffin, which he had set down on a torture table. Angel caught a whiff of blood, but not fresh—enough had been spilled in that room that its unique tang had lasted over the centuries.

Even from behind, Angel recognized Obregon. His nice suit was lightly stained from his trip through the tunnels, his silver hair neatly combed. The table he stood before was made of heavy wood, polished to a high gloss, and large enough to hold a body. Leather straps were mostly decomposed but there was still enough remaining to see they once had been at both ends of the table to hold down arms and legs. The box that rested on the table was more ornate and, Angel knew, more dangerous.

He resisted the impulse to make some kind of quip, to let his prey know that he was coming, and charged into the room, leaping across the open space toward the old man. But Obregon heard, or sensed, something. He spun around and whipped out with both fists, smashing into Angel and throwing him off course. Instead of landing on Obregon, Angel hit the edge of the solid torture table and fell to the ground.

Obregon followed with a quick kick to Angel's jaw, snapping the vampire's head back into one of the table's legs. *This started out well,* Angel thought wryly as he struggled to gain his footing again. Obregon, seemingly even faster than he had been the first time they'd met, had already darted to a wall of ancient equipment and grabbed a long iron poker, which he held out before him like a sword.

Angel found his feet and faced the man. "You know that won't do you any good, right?" he asked with a dry chuckle.

Obregon whisked it through the space between them, so fast Angel couldn't even track it with his eyes. "Unless I behead you with it," he replied.

"Not very sharp," Angel pointed out.

A smile spread across Obregon's features. "I didn't say it would be painless." He slashed the other way, and Angel realized that he was moving it so fast there was indeed a possibility it could cut through Angel's flesh and bones. He needed a weapon of his own if he wanted to close with Obregon.

So instead of attacking, he retreated, circling around behind the torture table.

"Surely you don't think that's going to keep me at bay for long, do you?" Obregon asked.

"Doesn't need to," Angel said. Without telegraphing his intentions, he suddenly lowered himself, caught the bottom edge of the heavy table's surface, hoisted it off the ground, and hurled it at Obregon. The casket spun into the air. Whatever part of the old man the table didn't flatten Angel would be able to deal with easily.

But Obregon surprised him again, swatting the gigantic table aside as if it were a gnat. It crashed into a wall. Before Angel could even react, Obregon had scooped the small casket toward himself and picked it up.

"You underestimate me, vampire," he said. "I would have thought you'd have learned by now. You couldn't defeat me before—"

"You went into the sunlight," Angel reminded him.

"'All's fair,'" Obregon quoted. "You couldn't beat me before. Here, in this room, is where I achieved the height of my power. The necromantic rituals I performed here made me the strongest individual on the planet in my day. That's why I brought the casket and the key here, to be reunited with my power. Without even opening the casket I can already feel it coursing through me."

He knelt down, keeping the poker at the ready, and set the casket down on the ground before him. Then with his free hand he removed a small star-shaped object from his pocket. The key, Angel guessed.

Angel attacked again, closing the space between them with a single leap. But Obregon brought the poker up defensively and drove it through Angel's left shoulder and down into his chest. Angel screamed from the white-hot pain and retreated. Obregon laughed at the damage he'd done.

"That was just foolish," he said. "You can't hope to stop me, Angel. Why even try?"

Angel gripped his shoulder with his right hand as if he could contain the agony. First the gunshots, and now this. "It's what I do."

"I'll be sure to relieve you of that obligation momentarily," Obregon said. He applied the starburst key to a spot on the casket's lid. As Angel watched, unable to stop it, the lid opened itself and a fine, yellow mist drifted out. Angel hoped for a moment that it was the wrong box, that the man had just exposed himself to some kind of toxic agent. But that hope was dashed when Obregon stood tall and inhaled great lungfuls of the yellow stuff. His chest seemed to expand as he took it in, and a self-satisfied smirk appeared on his face. Within seconds the yellow mist had vanished from the air and Obregon had grown in size, seemingly becoming more youthful at the same time, his muscles straining the seams of his clothing. "That's much better," he said. "I feel like the old me again."

Angel was pretty sure this was a problem.

He wasn't quite sure how he was going to get around it, so he thought he'd try pride first. "I thought you wanted to prove you could beat me by yourself," he said. Even talking took a lot out of him, but he figured the longer he could make Obregon talk, the more chance he'd have that he could recover enough to take another shot at the guy. "Not the souped-up you, but the regular you. You think you can take me but you haven't stopped me yet."

Obregon simply smiled, apparently fully aware of Angel's tack. "I have nothing to prove," he said. "Not to you or anyone else. Even without my full power I was not driven by ego, and even less so now. What use does a god have for ego?"

Angel snorted a laugh. "Not driven by ego?" he repeated. "What about the fancy suits, the nice hair? You didn't need those things to find the key and the box. In fact, they probably slowed you down. I'm no psychologist, but if you're not all about ego, I'm Little Miss Muffet."

"And just how is that curds and whey?" Obregon asked in response. "I was never a fan, even in my younger days. And one thing I'll say for the Scholars, they do let their prisoners stay up-to-date. I've been locked away for centuries but I still watch the *Iron Chef*."

The iron who? Angel wondered. Before he could say anything else, though, Obregon's expression became stern. "Enough of this," he said, raising a hand toward Angel. "And enough of you. I have what I need, and you've become a nuisance. Good-bye."

He started for the door, and Angel forced himself to ignore the pain and move to block Obregon's path. But Obregon simply straight-armed him, stopping his attack cold. New agony lanced through Angel's being, and he fell back against a series of chains attached in varying lengths to the moldering walls. Obregon went through the opening into the tunnel and was gone.

Some time later—probably just a few seconds, he realized, though he couldn't have guaranteed it at that moment—he was able to see again, and the darkness that had closed around him drew back sufficiently for him to locate the doorway. He yanked a length of stout chain from the wall, the adobe tearing away easily under his effort. He wasn't sure what it would do against Obregon now, but any weapon was probably better than none.

He turned right out of the door, hands outstretched to keep his balance in the dark tunnel. He'd been able to see clearly before, but now the wrenching pain of his wounds had weakened his senses as well as his muscles.

He'd been traveling through the tunnel for a few minutes when he heard footsteps coming toward him. He braced himself for what he thought was coming, knowing that he was still too weak to beat Obregon, that he hadn't had a long enough recuperative period.

"Angel?" It wasn't Obregon after all.

"Mildred?" he said weakly. "Is that you?"

She came closer so that he could see her, even in the dark. She looked as if she'd aged another ten years in the past hour. "I followed him, Angel. But then I thought I should come back and get you, because following him by myself doesn't really do anyone much good."

"I was afraid he'd see you."

"No, I hid in an alcove. He wasn't looking, anyway—just stormed through as if he owned the place."

"He might as well." Angel hadn't admitted defeat yet, but he was willing to admit to being the underdog at this point.

"Anyway," she said, taking him by the sleeve and leading him like a lost boy, "I followed him outside. Then it got too strange out there, so I came back for you." He felt a twinge of discomfort, and noticed that in her free hand she clutched a crucifix, liberated from one of the mission's walls.

"You won't need that," he assured her.

"I'm sure I won't," she replied. "But better safe than sorry, right? Anyway, I wasn't sure if it really worked, or if it's just another story."

"It works. Just keep it away from me," he said. "And what do you mean, it's 'strange out there'?"

"You'll see in a minute," she said. "I'm not sure I can explain."

Angel didn't press her for more details, content to wait until they got out there. They weren't far now from where they had come down into the tunnels, and Angel picked up the pace as he got closer and the urgency built within him. Once Obregon left the mission grounds, he would have any number of potential victims, and it would be even harder for Angel to find and stop him.

When they reached the narrow, worn staircase that led up out of the depths, Mildred touched his arm again. "You're badly hurt," she said. "I saw what he did to you in there."

Angel shrugged, and winced at the shooting pain when he did. "Can't let it stop me, though."

"Somehow I didn't think you would."

He didn't answer, just raced up the steps and through the cluttered storeroom in which he'd found them, bursting through the door into the outside.

And then he saw what she meant.

Obregon pulled the lightning to him.

He stood in the center of the plaza—the plaza that had once been the central point of his own personal empire—and raised his hands to the incandescent sky. In humble obeisance, bolts of pure fire leaped to his fingertips. With a smile, he accepted the electrical charge that coursed through him as their offering.

He believed that his power had grown since the last time he had felt this way. Whether it was his new maturity, a result of the years in solitary confinement with nothing but his own thoughts to occupy him, or something about Los Angeles in the new century that accentuated the power he contained, he didn't know. But he liked the way it felt. He was omnipotent, he thought, or close to it.

With a wave of his hand he bade the grass bow toward him, and it did. With a glance he willed one of the mission's exterior walls to collapse. It complied without hesitation. Adobe that had withstood earthquakes and fire, wind and rain and hail, simply crumbled at Obregon's unspoken command.

This, he thought, *this is the way I was meant to live. Not penned like an animal, but free and in control.*

And then, from someplace behind him, he sensed the vampire's return. *A minor nuisance now. But a nuisance just the same.* He turned to deliver the killing blow.

Angel saw Obregon turning toward him, but then something else caught his eye, beyond Obregon, approaching from the breezeway that led to the outlying buildings. Wesley came first, followed by Gunn, Lorne, and Fred, and then the two Scholars he'd knocked out earlier. At first he thought Cordelia brought up the rear, but then he saw that she was accompanied by the sleeping ranger, who wasn't asleep anymore. He wasn't sure what they could do to help, but at this point he'd take all the assistance he could get.

"Obregon!" Wesley shouted, drawing the man's attention to him. His tone was firm, commanding. "You might just as well give up now!"

Obregon looked at Wesley and his companions, then glanced back at Angel with a bemused expression. "You brought friends," he said. "How delightful."

Angel hadn't, but saw no reason to disabuse Obregon of the notion. "He's right," Angel said. "I'd surrender, if I were you."

"I think not," Obregon answered. "I have my full powers again. There's nothing you can do—"

"You have been beaten before," the slender Scholar pointed out. "It will happen again."

Obregon let his gaze wander over the ragtag group assembled before him. "You are mistaken," he said simply. Then he raised his hands into the air. Lightning flashed to him—Angel smelled its ozone scent, sharp and biting, and felt the blast of heat—and as Obregon worked it like a baker with dough, it grew in brilliance and size.

When it had reached what Obregon must have considered the right size, he hurled it. Angel felt the heat as the lightning streaked toward him like a miniature sun. But one of the Scholars threw up a mystical shield, and the ball of light burst against it, sending licks of flame all over the plaza, illuminating the statue of Father Serra like a flash bulb. The other Scholar followed up with a spell of his own. Within moments the plaza became a magickal battleground, with spells and mystical attacks flying in every direction. It seemed that Angel and Gunn were the only ones sitting the battle out. Gunn stood off to one side, his ax in his hands, looking as if he wished there were something he could hack at but knowing that the others had a better handle on this kind of thing than he did.

But Obregon seemed capable of absorbing or shaking off everything they threw at him. And his own attacks gained in fury as the minutes ticked by, until Angel worried that his friends had underestimated Obregon's power.

There was just one thing to do, then.

His shoulder and chest still hurt, but he could bite the pain back, ignore it for a few moments. If mystical attacks wouldn't take out Obregon, there had to be a physical way to do it. While Obregon was distracted, he leaped, throwing the length of chain he still carried around the sorcerer's neck and pulling it tight.

Obregon's eyes bulged out at Angel's attack. He clawed at the chain, but the others kept up their magickal assault. Obregon seemed to have a hard time battling on two fronts. Angel saw the ancient links bite deep into the flesh of the man's throat.

But then he felt powerful hands on his own neck. Obregon was fighting back after all. His fingers were like steel rods. Angel couldn't be strangled,

ANGEL

but as with the poker earlier, if Obregon simply tore through his neck and decapitated him that would be the end of it. He couldn't let go of the chain to peel his foe's fingers away from his neck without losing whatever momentum he had gained.

So the question, he knew, was which one of them would go first? Or would it be simultaneous?

He kept up the pressure on the chain, but the piercing agony at his neck was nearly too much. He felt consciousness waver. The plaza began to go dark and tilt crazily, like something from a funhouse ride. Images appeared in his mind's eye, replacing what he could no longer see of the mission grounds. His parents, when he was very young. Darla, blond and lovely, teaching him the dark joys of bloodlust. A progression of other women over the years—lovers, victims, often both. Then Buffy, who had reminded him of a champion's duty, and shown him how to love. Finally Cordelia Chase, whose beauty spread from within her and encompassed everything she came close to.

I'm losing it, Angel thought, as even the image of Cordelia shimmered and blurred, like a reflection on a still pool after a stone has been tossed into it. *He's going to win.*

In desperate hope that it would give him renewed strength, Angel summoned up the picture of Cordelia again—then a succession of them: Cordy at a party, dancing, fighting, sitting with

Angel in the courtyard of the hotel. As his flesh parted and rational thought was driven from his mind he thought he could even hear her voice. "To me!" it seemed she was shouting. "Touch me! Put your hands on me!"

Okay, he thought, and his world went dark. His hands started to relax their grip on the chain....

Suddenly Obregon screamed and released him. Angel fell to the ground, startled, as the sorcerer bucked in pain. Glancing back toward the door, Angel could see Cordelia, a white aura glowing around her like a bridal veil. Lorne, Fred, Wes, and the two Scholars all had their hands on her, and waves of mystical energy washed from them like blue flames, licking across their bodies as it surged toward Cordy. She wasn't a higher being anymore, Angel knew, but she was at least part demon, and maybe something about that made her the natural conduit for these energies. Channeled through Cordy's glow, the white aura grew, lighting the whole plaza like brightest day. For just a moment Angel worried that it was a kind of daylight, which would kill him, but that fear was groundless.

As Angel watched, fighting for consciousness, the very earth of the plaza seemed to buckle and writhe. *Earthquake?* he wondered. But it wasn't that. There was no shaking motion, no side to side. Instead something was emerging from under the ground. He corrected his first impression a second later—many somethings.

He tried to scramble out of their way, but quickly realized it wasn't necessary. They had no form, no physical substance, and simply passed through him like so many ghosts. They rose up like fast-growing crops, like burrowing animals released from earthen pens, hundreds of them from every part of the mission grounds. Their clothing was primitive by modern standards— baggy pants that looked like burlap, loose-fitting shirts tied at the waist with colorful sashes. Some didn't even wear shirts, and a few only had loincloths covering them. Most had headbands holding back long, straight black hair.

They were silent as they blossomed from the ground, but their expressions spoke volumes. They saw Obregon, pointed, and gesticulated. Angel would have sworn they conversed but there wasn't a sound—even the pounding winds had fallen silent, held back, he supposed, by the light that emanated from his friends.

And as they closed on Obregon—as his expression changed from smug satisfaction to sheer terror, Angel realized what he was seeing. These were Obregon's victims, the people who had died here to give him his power in the first place, or simply because of his insanity. They had lain there for centuries, waiting for a chance to have their revenge.

Now Angel could see their wounds—gaping, bleeding holes where they had been impaled on stakes, burn scars from the torch, slashes and stab wounds from swords and spears. In spite of those horrific wounds—*or because of them, really,* he thought; *likely no one who died peacefully of old age has come back*—they closed around Obregon, who turned this way and that in the center of the plaza, spinning as if to block whoever made the first move on him. He tried to gather lightning, to release mystical attacks, but his powers were completely subsumed by the bright white glow that grew from where Cordelia and the others stood.

Then the spirits of the restless dead reached him, and Obregon tried to fight them off, flailing his arms. His mouth opened and a plaintive scream rolled out. Angel did his best to ignore it. He didn't like to see anyone in that kind of torment, but better Obregon than his next thousand victims. The Indians closed ranks, and after a few moments Angel couldn't even see Obregon anymore. The Indians were soundless still. Obregon fell quiet too, and the whole scene played out before him as if on a silent movie screen.

After a little while Angel realized their ranks were thinning. It seemed that whenever one of the Indians touched Obregon, taking his or her revenge in whatever small way, he or she just blinked from existence. Only a few minutes after it had filled, the plaza emptied out, except for the still, battered form of Obregon. While Angel watched, the white glow began to fade, and as it did the tableau formed by his teammates broke up.

Angel rubbed his ragged throat. "Is that . . . is it over?" he asked, his voice hoarse. It hurt to talk, but then, it hurt to exist. Didn't mean he wasn't glad he did. Sort of.

Cordelia favored him with her smile. "Looks like it," she replied. She took in the other participants with a wave of her hand. "Some pretty powerful magicks here, from some experienced spellcasters. Channeled through one being, they're far more effective than when used individually. I don't think Obregon will be a problem again. But just in case, we'll put *him* in the box this time. 'His' power was just power, diffuse in its natural state. Without him to concentrate it I don't think it'll trouble us anymore."

"You're . . . you're incredible," Angel managed.

"Pretty much, huh?" Cordy acknowledged. "But, not to sound too much like I'm accepting the Oscar I'll never win, couldn't have done it without the little people. Like you."

"Me?" Angel asked.

"He had us, Angel. We couldn't get the edge. If you hadn't jumped him, weakened him, even Higher Being Girl couldn't have done anything."

Angel nodded. It made a certain amount of

sense, he guessed, and anyway he didn't want to think he'd been extraneous. He caught the eye of the slender Scholar. "Sorry I . . . um . . ."

"Quite all right," the man said. "We don't blame you a bit."

"I revived them," Wesley explained. "I figured we'd need all the help we could get, and after all, we did have a common foe in Obregon."

"Right," Angel said. His strength was coming back to him, though it would be some time before he was back to normal. "But killing people in my city? Not acceptable."

"Won't happen again," the Scholar assured him. "It was regrettably necessary."

"If I even *think* it's going to happen again, I won't be so merciful," Angel said. Talking tough was difficult when the skin of his throat hung in shreds, but he thought he'd made his point. "I should kill you out of principle, but since you helped vanquish Obregon I'm feeling generous. Just catch the first flight out of here and don't come back."

"Happy to," the larger one put in. "Ghastly weather here anyway."

Mildred and the Scholars started for the torture chamber then, to get the casket that would contain what was left of Obregon. Angel stood beside Cordelia, watching them, remembering how she had given him strength to fight the sorcerer.

Remembering, too, how distant she had been since returning from her time away, and that she would be sleeping at Connor's place tonight and not the Hyperion. He had battled Obregon because it was what he did. She had helped, not out of love for Angel, but because it was what she did.

"Cor," he said weakly.

"Angel?"

"Give me a hand, here?"

She hooked an arm around his waist and helped him toward the parking lot. "He munched you up good, didn't he?"

Angel breathed in her scent, enjoyed the closeness of her, and nodded. "Yeah," he said. "I might need you to help me out for a while. Can you do that?"

She snickered, and he thought she knew exactly what he was up to. But she didn't let him go. "Sure," she said, her voice so soft that only he could hear. "I can do that."

"I'm trying to comprehend this," Angel heard Gene Kinross saying as they all assembled in the mission's parking lot. "Computers you can fit on your desk? And they can talk to one another?"

"That's right, essentially," Wesley told him.

"Not talk, exactly," Fred corrected. "Well, some of them can, I guess, with voice recognition and speech simulation software."

"Hey, kiddies, don't try to catch him all up at once," Lorne objected. "First things first. He should be warned about telemarketers, reality TV, and boy bands before you get all technical on him."

Cordelia had insisted that Angel try to walk on his own. He managed, with some difficulty, and when he stopped to lean on his car he overheard Gunn talking to Mildred, who had returned after directing the Scholars. "So what do you think, Mildred?" he asked her. "You ready to join up full time?"

"Oh, heavens no, I don't think so," she said. Angel straightened and looked at her over the top of the car. She was beaming at being asked.

"We couldn't have done it without you," Angel assured her. "You really closed the case, in a lot of ways."

"Well, I don't know about that," she said. "I'm sure you'd have figured it out. And . . . well, I don't mean to be judgmental, but I'm not sure I want to work with . . . well, you know . . ."

"Vampires?" Angel offered.

Gunn laughed. "He may be a vamp, but he's one of the good ones. Maybe the best."

"I'm sure he is," Mildred said, blushing at the idea that she might have insulted him. "But still . . . it's very different from the books, you know?"

"Maybe," Gunn suggested, "you've just been readin' the wrong books."

"There's a lot less running around and fighting in drafty old missions and more sitting around, reasoning out the answers over nice cups of tea, in the ones I like," Mildred said. "I think perhaps I'll stick to those. And I'm sure Pookie would approve."

"Can't argue with Pookie," Angel said to her. "But thanks for your help, just the same." With some effort he raised his voice so everyone present could hear him. "Thanks to all of you, for what you did. I appreciate it."

He spoke to everyone, but his eyes were on Cordelia. She acknowledged his look, flashed him a smile, and got in her car. Lorne had already taken the driver's seat of the GTX, since Angel was in no condition to drive, but Fred and Gunn climbed in with Cordelia. In a moment she was racing away down the road, back toward Los Angeles. Back toward home.

She was, he knew, putting some distance between them. He hoped he'd be able to catch up.

Someday.

ABOUT THE AUTHOR

Jeff Mariotte is the author of several previous Angel novels, including *Close to the Ground, Hollywood Noir, Haunted,* and *Stranger to the Sun.* With Nancy Holder he wrote the Buffy/Angel crossover trilogy *Unseen* and the Angel novel *Endangered Species*, and with Maryelizabeth Hart added to the mix the nonfiction *Angel: The Casefiles: Volume 1*. He's published several other books, including the original horror novel *The Slab*, and more comic books than he has time to count, some of which have been nominated for Stoker and International Horror Guild awards. With his wife, the aforementioned Maryelizabeth Hart, and partner Terry Gilman, he co-owns Mysterious Galaxy, a bookstore specializing in science fiction, fantasy, mystery, and horror. He lives in San Diego, California, with his family and pets, in a home filled with books, music, toys, and other examples of American pop culture. More information than you would ever want to know about him is at www.jeffmariotte.com.